"What's Your Name?"

J.T. asked the woman who'd arrived on his doorstep in the middle of a blizzard.

"I don't know," she whispered.

J.T. strained to hear the words. "How'd you get here?"

"I guess my car skidded off the road and into a ditch. I walked from there. My head hurts."

"I'll call the doctor right away. You're going to have to trust me," he added.

"I'm also…pregnant."

J.T.'s eyes zoomed in on her very large belly. She'd walked half a mile in a snowstorm in her condition? His gaze slid up to her face. Shock spread fast and far inside him.

He knew her. The very pregnant woman without a memory was Gina Banning, a part of his past that he'd almost laid to rest.…

ROMANCE

Dear Reader,

Silhouette is celebrating its 20th anniversary throughout 2000! So, to usher in the first summer of the millennium, why not indulge yourself with six powerful, passionate, provocative love stories from Silhouette Desire?

Jackie Merritt returns to Desire with a MAN OF THE MONTH who's *Tough To Tame*. Enjoy the sparks that fly between a rugged ranch manager and the feisty lady who turns his world upside down! Another wonderful romance from RITA Award winner Caroline Cross is in store for you this month with *The Rancher and the Nanny*, in which a rags-to-riches hero learns trust and love from the riches-to-rags woman who cares for his secret child.

Watch for Meagan McKinney's *The Cowboy Meets His Match*—an octogenarian matchmaker sets up an ice-princess heiress with a virile rodeo star. The Desire theme promotion THE BABY BANK, about sperm-bank client heroines who find love unexpectedly, concludes with Susan Crosby's *The Baby Gift*. Wonderful newcomer Sheri WhiteFeather offers another irresistible Native American hero with *Cheyenne Dad*. And Kate Little's hero reunites with his lost love in a marriage of convenience to save her from financial ruin in *The Determined Groom*.

So come join in the celebration and start your summer off on the supersensual side—by reading all six of these tantalizing Desire books!

Enjoy!

Joan Marlow Golan

Joan Marlow Golan
Senior Editor, Silhouette Desire

Please address questions and book requests to:
Silhouette Reader Service
U.S.: 3010 Walden Ave., P.O. Box 1325, Buffalo, NY 14269
Canadian: P.O. Box 609, Fort Erie, Ont. L2A 5X3

The Baby Gift

SUSAN CROSBY

Published by Silhouette Books

America's Publisher of Contemporary Romance

For Debbie Swanson, who so graciously shares her daughter with me, with love and admiration for the amazing person you are.

And for Melissa Jeglinski once again.
My stalwart editor. You're simply the best.

SILHOUETTE BOOKS

ISBN 0-373-76301-8

THE BABY GIFT

Copyright © 2000 by Susan Bova Crosby

Books by Susan Crosby

Silhouette Desire

The Mating Game #888
Almost a Honeymoon #952
Baby Fever #1018
Wedding Fever #1061
Marriage on His Mind #1108
Bride Candidate #9 #1131
His Most Scandalous Secret #1158
His Seductive Revenge #1162
His Ultimate Temptation #1186
†*The Groom's Revenge* #1214
The Baby Gift #1301

*The Lone Wolves
†Fortune's Children: The Brides

SUSAN CROSBY

believes in the value of setting goals, but also in the magic of making wishes. Ascribing to the theory that the "harder you work, the luckier you get," she has been fortunate enough to receive *Romantic Times Magazine*'s Reviewers' Choice Award for Best Silhouette Desire of the Year, as well as being a finalist for the Romance Writers of America RITA Award. Her books appear regularly on the bestseller lists.

Susan earned a B.A. in English while raising her sons, now grown. She and her husband live in the central valley of California, the land of wine grapes, asparagus and almonds. Her checkered past includes jobs as a synchronized swimming instructor, personnel interviewer at a toy factory and trucking company manager, but her current occupation as a writer is her all-time favorite.

Readers are welcome to write to her at P.O. Box 1836, Lodi, CA 95241.

IT'S OUR 20th ANNIVERSARY!
We'll be celebrating all year,
Continuing with these fabulous titles,
On sale in June 2000.

One

Police Chief J.T. Ryker couldn't sleep. He supposed it was the quiet that had awakened him, a sense of something being different. His heart wasn't thundering from the old nightmare but from an indefinable sensation—like holding your breath and listening hard, anticipation building and building until it just had to explode.

J.T. no longer questioned gut feelings. He climbed out of bed and looked out the window. Three hours ago he'd overseen the town's less-raucous-than-usual New Year's Eve celebration that ended at precisely midnight when snow began to fall.

What filled his sight now was a blizzard.

He ignored his uniform in favor of warmer clothes, then headed out the door with Deputy, the beagle he'd inherited with the job. He carried the dog through the snow until they reached Main Street, then Deputy led the way, happy for a middle-of-the-night trek through town. Protected by a wooden awning, they patrolled their little corner of the world, making sure it was safe.

The dog's nails clip-clip-clipped along the wood-plank walkway of downtown. Accustomed to his owner's routine, the beagle stopped at the first shop and pressed his nose to the glass door. J.T. turned the handle and sighed. Mrs. Foley had left the front door to her fabric, craft and ladies' undergarments shop unlocked again, even though he'd reminded her at midnight. Three doors down, in Aaron Taylor's hardware and auto parts store, no telltale red beam flashed. Aaron hadn't activated the security alarm—again.

J.T. tried to educate them, but they remained blissfully stubborn about potential dangers, no matter how farfetched the possibility. The biggest crime they'd seen recently was a spate of graffiti vandalism, and that hard-boiled perpetrator had been identified by his mother, who'd recognized his handwriting and dragged him in to accept his punishment.

It was a far cry from J.T.'s nine years on the L.A.P.D. A year's worth of crime in this mountain community wouldn't fill a week's log in the smallest L.A. substation. It suited J.T. just fine, especially since he was the only paid police officer, as well as the fire chief and all-around public servant. In a town of 514 residents, with houses scattered over miles of varying terrain, he never had a dull moment. He couldn't remember the last time he'd taken a day off. In September, maybe?

Hunching against the wind, he stuck his hands deeper in his jacket pockets. "A little trip to the tropics sound good to you?" he asked the dog trotting beside him. "Want to get out of that dumb-looking sweater and into a pair of swim trunks?"

Deputy barked once—J.T. always took that as a yes—then the dog went still as a post, his ears pricked up. After a couple of seconds he charged off.

J.T. looked ahead and spotted a heap in front of his office. Old John, he supposed. Too drunk to know he could die of hypothermia on a night like this. Too drunk to pick up the phone hanging by the office door, a direct line to J.T. at home.

Deputy's tail wagged like a metronome at top speed, his rear end moving almost as fast. A woman's soft laughter drifted with the wind as J.T. neared his office.

"I'm awake, dog. Stop licking my face."

Her words were low, but not slurred like those of someone freezing to death.

"Stop it, you idiot." She laughed again, taking the sting from her command.

Deputy barked and bounded toward J.T., then returned to the huddled woman again almost instantly.

J.T. crouched in front of her, resisting shining his flashlight when she shied away from him. An overhead light illuminated her red jacket, but a fuzzy-trimmed hood shadowed her face. With a violent shiver she pulled Deputy closer.

"Hi," J.T. said.

She seemed to get smaller.

"That unfriendly pup in your arms is Deputy, and I'm the police chief, J.T. Ryker."

"Oh." She waved a hand toward the sign overhead, but she seemed to keep her focus directly on him. "Then you're who I've been waiting for."

Her teeth chattered, which was all he could see of her face. A muffler covered her chin.

"How long have you been here?" J.T. asked.

Her shoulders shifted in a decidedly uncasual shrug. She petted Deputy as he wriggled in her arms. "I used the phone, but there was no answer."

Which meant she couldn't have been waiting more than ten minutes. "Would you like to go inside?"

A few beats passed. "Do you have identification?" she asked.

He hesitated long enough that he could feel her withdraw. It had been almost three years since someone hadn't taken his word at face value—since the day he'd taken the job. He pulled his leather badge holder from his pocket, then passed it to her. She turned it over and over in her gloved hands.

"There's photo ID inside the wallet," he said, sensing a more-than-average wariness. He wondered how old she was. A teenage runaway? A woman needing police protection? Or was she just lost—and rightfully suspicious of a man out walking at 3:00 a.m., even one claiming to be a police officer.

"What's your name?" he asked.

Seconds ticked by as he waited. Even the dog noticed the tension in the air and backed away from her, his head cocked. Finally she whispered, "I don't know."

J.T. strained to hear the words. "How'd you get here?"

"I guess my car skidded off the road and into a ditch. That's where I was when I came to, anyway. I walked from there. About half a mile, according to a sign I saw along the way."

"Were you in the driver's seat?"

She nodded, then slid a hand along the inside of her hood. "Where am I?"

"Lost and Found."

Her reaction was slow to come. "I'm...lost and found?"

"The name of the town. I know. It threw me for a loop the first time I heard it, too."

"Is it in California?"

"Yes. You're about three thousand feet up in the Sierra Nevada mountains in the north-central part of the state. The closest big city is Sacramento, and that's an hour and a half's drive. Come on, let's get you inside so you can warm up." He held out a hand to her.

"My head hurts."

"I'll call the doctor right away. You're going to have to trust me," he added.

"I'm also—" she reached for his hand "—pregnant." She wobbled as she stood.

J.T. steadied her, his eyes zeroing in on her very pregnant belly unprotected by her jacket, obviously not designed as maternity wear. She'd walked half a mile in a snowstorm in her condition?

"I'm okay now," she said, pulling her hand free.

His gaze slid up to her face. Shock lit an inferno inside him that spread fast and far. Sweat turned impossibly icy beneath the layers of his clothes.

He knew her. The very pregnant woman without a memory was Gina Banning, a part of his past that he'd almost laid to rest.

In their first conversation she'd tried to tease him into telling her what his initials stood for. In their last, she'd told him she hated him.

Then a week later she'd married his partner.

She didn't know what to make of the man, J.T. Ryker. One minute he was all kindness and concern, the next he was staring at her with cold, hard eyes. He'd taken her directly to the clinic, a few doors down from his office, because the heat was always left on there, he said.

She burrowed into the blanket he'd wrapped around her as they waited for the doctor to arrive. The police chief paced.

Back and forth he walked, sending a glance her way now and then as if he was knotted up with questions but had lost his ability to speak. The more she watched him, the more her head hurt.

Who am I? The biggest question of all hung over her like a lead blanket, the weight of it almost unbearable.

To distract herself she focused on the man. Early to midthirties, she guessed. Old enough to have character in his face. Experience. Tall, broad-shouldered and slim-hipped; strong enough to subdue someone without drawing the gun at his side. He'd tossed his jacket and gloves into one of a dozen pink plastic chairs in the waiting room as soon as he'd cocooned her in the blanket, his sharp-jawed face almost terrifyingly fierce—at odds with a voice he kept gentle. His eyes were a golden-brown, shades lighter than his hair. His frown lines seemed a part of him.

She wished she knew why he'd turned angry.

So much confused her. Answers to endless questions floated just outside her ability to recall. Each time she tried to pluck one out of the turmoil in her mind, her head pounded. Worst of all, the baby hadn't moved since…since she didn't know when.

Yanking off her gloves, she spread her hands over her belly, then spotted a gold wedding band on her left hand. Someone must be missing her—her husband, the father of her baby. Surely he would track her down and fill in her memory gaps. She twisted the band around her finger again and again, not finding the comfort she thought it would bring.

The baby rolled.

"Oh!" The sound escaped her, surprise and relief.

"Did you remember something?" the chief asked, stopping in front of her. Deputy had been sleeping under a nearby chair. He lifted his head and seemed to be waiting, too.

"My baby moved." Tears stung her eyes. "I've been so worried."

His gaze settled on her belly, where her hands formed a protective shield. He touched her ring. "You're married."

"Well, of course I'm married," she snapped back. "I'm pregnant."

"One doesn't necessarily rule out the other," he said, a bit of a smile relaxing his features.

"It does with me."

"How do you know that?"

She frowned. "I just do. Some things you don't forget."

He crouched in front of her. "What's your name?"

His expression had turned all fierce again, his gaze drilling her. She pressed her fingers to her forehead. "I don't know."

"This is no time for an interrogation, J.T."

The voice came from a doorway leading from the waiting room into the inner offices. She opened her eyes and watched a man of about the chief's age move silently into the room. Sympathetic eyes, hair a little on the shaggy side, whipcord lean body. He nudged the chief aside, then knelt in front of her. His hands weren't soft as they clasped hers, but they soothed, anyway. She almost melted into the chair.

"I'm Dr. Max Hunter, and I'm going to take care of you."

"Okay," she whispered, her throat tightening. "Thank you."

J.T. watched the exchange, his tension draining. Max had that effect on people. Born to heal. How Lost and Found had gotten lucky enough to have him settle there was a miracle in itself. He wasn't much younger than J.T.'s thirty-four years, but he seemed to have lived three lifetimes.

Peripherally he heard Max question Gina. She tensed up again as he asked about her memory. Although Max's questions were asked kindly, J.T. saw distress in her face when she darted a look at him.

"We've pretty much determined she can't recall anything personal, Max."

The doctor stood. "We'll do an ultrasound and see just how that baby's doing. Wait here a couple of minutes while I get the room ready." He squeezed her shoulder before he left.

J.T. stepped forward. "I'll leave you in Max's competent hands—"

"No!" She grabbed his shirtsleeve. "What if my memory comes back and you're not here?"

He reminded himself to treat her like any other victim. "I have to get to your car. You must have a wallet or something with identification. Deputy will keep you company."

She stared out the window, then dragged her hood back at last, freeing a cloud of shiny, dark-brown hair, static electricity making it seem alive. Eyes as dark as her hair settled on him, the sparkle he remembered dulled now with pain and worry.

He should take a lesson from her in moving on, because she'd obviously put the past behind her. He'd only deluded himself into thinking he had—the ball of fire in his stomach told him otherwise.

"How can you find my car in a storm like this?"

"It's my job." He was afraid she'd left someone behind, either in the car or, worse, outside in the snow. It wasn't a task that could wait until the storm stopped—or until daybreak. He scooped up his jacket from the chair and slipped it on. "Do you have your keys?"

"I think I left them in the car."

He questioned her about landmarks and direction until Max came into the room, saying he was ready for her. J.T. waited for her to disappear into the exam room before he pulled the doctor aside.

"I know her, Max. Her name is Gina Banning—or at least it was Banning three years ago, which was the last time I saw her. Her husband was my last partner at the L.A.P.D. He died in a car accident right before I left the force. Gina was with him and was critically injured. She spent a month in the hospital."

"Ah."

"Meaning?"

"Meaning her amnesia could very well be caused and sustained by a flashback to that accident rather than by blunt trauma or concussion. Could be both in combination, too. I'll know more after I examine her." He cocked his head at J.T. "Why didn't you tell her who she is?"

"I started to, then she looked at me without the

slightest recognition, and I didn't know whether it would hurt more than help. What do you think?''

"I think you made a good decision. If she needs to hide behind the amnesia for a while, we need to let her. Her memory will likely return when she can handle the consequences of living through the accident again.''

"But she must have a new husband worried sick about her. Obviously she remarried.''

Max frowned. "I'm not schooled enough in amnesia to know what could come of having someone confront her and try to force her memory, but I'll research it. And I agree that we have an obligation to notify her family.''

Her family. The words lingered in J.T.'s mind as he walked home to get his official vehicle, a four-wheel-drive sports utility vehicle. Reeling from the memories brought back by Gina's reappearance, he debated whether to call out a couple of his volunteer cadets, then decided to give it one shot by himself first.

He shut down the clamoring pieces of his past as he searched for her car, grateful he had a job to do. She'd skidded off the opposite side of the road, she'd said, into a shallow ditch, knocking her head against the driver's side window or frame. Something had told her to stay put—that it was her best chance for survival. But something stronger had urged her out of the car and up the road as the snow started coming down harder. After a couple of minutes walking, she'd seen a sign advertising Cochran's Food & Fuel, 1/2 Mile.

J.T. slowed from a crawl to a creep when he caught a lucky glimpse of the sign. Lost and Found didn't often get snow, and seldom in this amount, but once or twice a winter the area took on the magical look of a Christmas card, rarely lasting more than a day or two. He wished this hadn't been one of those rare days.

Rounding a bend, he saw her car just off the road, a few inches of fresh powder muting the red color. The rear bumper cleared the road, but was still dangerously close. Had she stayed in the car, she might have been clipped by a passing vehicle—if she even survived the night.

He turned on his flashing ambers, then positioned his Explorer to make use of his headlights and spotlight before approaching her car. No chains. He gritted his teeth. She was damned lucky to have gone off the road where she did. At several spots along the route the drop-off was sheer and deadly.

What the hell had she been thinking, driving in the mountains in winter, in snow, without snow tires or chains? Why would she do such an idiotic thing? She was a good seven hours from home, driving in the dead of night, in unfamiliar territory. He couldn't imagine what could have prompted such a suicide run.

Was she looking for *him?* He didn't believe in co-incidences, and no other possibility seemed feasible. *Another impulsive decision, Gina?*

Furious he might be on target with his suspicion, he jerked open the driver's door of her roomy sedan. At least she had sense enough to drive a solid car, one known for safety. The deflated airbag sagged against the steering wheel, its lifesaving mission accomplished. Her keys dangled from the ignition. He snatched her big purse from the floor of the passenger seat, then carried it back to his truck and upended the contents onto the driver's seat.

The mysteries of woman spilled onto the uphol-stery—crumpled tissues, sunglasses, an economy-size package of gum with three pieces missing, lipstick, hand cream, prenatal vitamins. A perfume atomizer, the flowery scent clinging to it. A map folded to the local route. He stuffed the items back into her purse.

He found cash in a manila envelope—almost three thousand dollars.

With a low whistle he opened her wallet. Four credit cards and a driver's license, all under the name Gina Banning.

The unexpectedness of it made J.T. lean against the car and stare sightlessly into the night. She hadn't re-married? That didn't make sense. He knew for a fact she wasn't the type to get pregnant out of wedlock and not marry the man responsible. Even without her memory she had known that much about herself. "As loyal as a puppy," her late husband said of her once. "And as blindly trusting."

Eric Banning's expertise had been in playing to peo-ple's weaknesses, a dubious skill which had sometimes worked to his benefit in police work. Hell, he had learned early on how to take advantage of what J.T. considered his strength—his unfaltering sense of duty and responsibility—managing somehow to turn it into a weakness. J.T. wondered if Eric had used Gina's blind trust against her somehow. Apparently she'd trusted another man, too. And J.T., as well, even though she didn't remember him…

Which could be the result of trauma, of course, and the fact he was the first person to come along and help her.

None of it added up. She wore a wedding ring, yet her husband had died three years ago. She was preg-nant, yet she wouldn't be pregnant without being mar-ried.

Three thousand dollars.

J.T. slapped her wallet rhythmically against the car door frame. What critical piece of information was he missing?

He hiked back to her car and popped open the trunk. Clothes were strewn everywhere, some still on hangers, as if she'd scooped them out of the closet and drawers, then dropped them in the trunk. A Sears bag overflowed with baby clothes and blankets, the tags attached. He dug out the receipt. She'd purchased everything yesterday at 5:18 p.m. in Bakersfield. Newborn disposable diapers filled another bag.

She'd been in a hurry. A big hurry. And she planned to be gone until after the baby arrived.

Who are you running from, Gina Banning? Whose child do you carry?

And why the hell are you here in Lost and Found?

Feeling the chief's eyes on her like the bright beam of a spotlight, she stared at her driver's license. Gina Banning. She repeated the name in her head a few times, testing it. Twenty-two years old. Five foot four, 120 pounds. Without baby, obviously.

Eric. Her husband's name, according to a health plan card with both their names on it. She spun her wedding ring around her finger.

"I can't picture a man's face," she said to J.T. and the doctor, who both waited silently as she examined the contents of her purse. "Isn't that odd? Shouldn't I have some recollection of my husband? And why is my checking account in my name only? Marriage means sharing everything."

"More important," the chief said, "why would you leave home when you're less than a month away from giving birth? I'll head over to my office and run a missing person's report—''

''No! Please. What if I'm running from something?'' Her voice echoed, loud and desperate, intensifying the pounding in her head. ''Isn't that reason enough not to alert someone where I am?''

''I have a duty, Gina.''

''I'm of age. And isn't it your first duty to make sure I'm kept safe?''

''Someone is probably worried about you. Your family—''

''I don't feel married.'' The statement caught her off guard, even the mournful tone of it. She was married to Eric. He must be the father of the baby moving comfortingly inside her. What could have driven her from home? From him? ''What if I end up on the news?''

''Don't borrow trouble,'' the doctor said, placing his hands on hers. ''You're getting all worked up, which is the last thing you need. Your only job at the moment is to get some rest. This has been a traumatic night for you, but your memory is going to come back, and we'll figure everything out as soon as it does.''

''But where can I go?''

''You go with me,'' J.T. said.

She shook her head again and again. ''I can't impose on you. Surely there's a hotel.''

''No hotel. No bed and breakfast.''

''I don't feel right…''

''We have no idea what you're up against, Gina. It's safer this way.'' No other option was reasonable, even though it was the last thing he wanted to do. Certainly he didn't hold her responsible for Eric's failings, but she was linked with him, this widow of a man he despised—the man responsible for the nightmares that forced J.T. to quit the department, the nightmares that had haunted him long after.

The only consideration now was her need for protection. He would protect her, no matter what the consequences. But would there be a price to pay when she remembered him? One more reason for her to hate him, when she found out he'd kept her identity from her?

His brother must be laughing from heaven. Chiding. In his lucid moments Mark had accused him of living his first life in the days of chivalry, then never stepping fully into the modern world. "Face it," Mark had said often. "Chivalry's dead."

Well, J.T. believed in living by his own code. If that meant giving up the precarious tranquility he'd finally found, in order to offer peace of mind to an innocent woman about to give birth, so be it.

There were worse fates. And the decision got easier just looking at her pale face, at the strain he saw in her eyes. He owed her for the pain he'd caused, no matter how righteous his reasons had been.

Deputy nudged him with his muzzle. J.T. realized that Max had helped Gina into her coat, and they were waiting for him.

After she was buckled into his car, he headed around to the driver's side. Max stopped him at the rear of the vehicle.

"Are you sure you can handle this?"

The quiet concern in his voice gave J.T. pause. "I have to, Max."

"There are plenty of people who would take her in."

"I would worry." He pulled up his sheepskin collar to warm his ears. "This is the best solution."

"She's more than just the widow of an old partner. I can see that."

"Leave it alone." Okay, so he'd been drawn to her all those years ago. To her laughter and sweetness. To the adoring glances toward Eric. She was everything he'd wanted but didn't dare to wish for.

Eric Banning hadn't deserved her.

"I'll stop by tomorrow," Max said, resting his hand on J.T.'s shoulder. "Call me if she shows any signs at all of going into labor, or if her headache gets worse. Or if the moon turns purple."

J.T. smiled. "Wondering if I was paying attention?"

Max made a noncommittal sound, then took a couple of steps back. "She'll try to maintain her independence. It seems extremely important to her."

"I'll let her think she's in charge."

"I'm not some helpless female," Gina called out the car window.

Both men turned in surprise. J.T. hadn't heard the window go down.

"This ought to be entertaining," Max murmured.

Hot air blasted J.T. as he climbed into the car. He started to adjust the heater to a more comfortable level, then hesitated. "You warm enough?" he asked.

"I don't need to be coddled."

The kitten had transformed into a tigress. He sent her a curious look. She stared straight out the window.

"I appreciate your giving me a place to stay, and I'll reimburse you for any expenses you incur. But I'm not an invalid. I'm not incompetent. And I'm certainly not witless. I *am* confused. Please don't make it worse by treating me like a child." She drew a sharp breath. "I've said that to someone before. I was mad then, too."

He remembered the moment as if it were yesterday.

She went silent as they drove the short distance to his house, then said suddenly, "My maiden name was Benedetto." She pressed a hand to her mouth and looked at him. "How do I know that? And I have brothers and sisters. I remember them. I remember!"

He pulled into the garage, then angled toward her in time to see her push her fingers against her forehead, a signal he'd come to recognize.

It occurred to him that she might remember *him* before she remembered whoever she was running from—or even before she recalled her late husband. He eyed her thoughtfully. Oh, yeah. She was bound to be plenty mad at being kept in the dark. Added to whatever had driven her from home in the first place, there could be bitter consequences all around.

But weren't some memories best left buried? If he'd had the chance to forget some things forever…

And yet it was his duty to help her remember, even as he hoped she never did.

He opened his car door. "Don't push it, Gina. It'll all come back on its own."

J.T. helped her out of the car, keeping a hand under her elbow as they entered the house. He looked around, trying to see it from her perspective. He'd banished a lot of his frustrations with a saw and hammer while turning this house into a home.

She didn't seem to look at her surroundings, however. Exhaustion lined her face. He guided her into the living room and settled her in a chair.

"Just relax for a minute while I get your stuff out of my car and make the guest room ready for you, okay?"

He thought she nodded.

"Okay, Gina? I don't want to be accused of treating you like a child."

She looked right at him, cool as snowfall, and he smiled. They'd almost been friends once upon a time. He focused on that.

After three trips he'd carted all of her belongings to the guest room. He folded back the blankets, then carried her toiletries into the adjoining bathroom, one she would share with him because he didn't want her out of earshot, in case she needed anything.

He returned to the living room and stopped short. What a picture she made, asleep sitting up. He couldn't begin to imagine the toll this day had taken on her. Every protective instinct flared. Whoever had pushed her into such a dire situation better hope he didn't show up soon. J.T. couldn't guarantee he wouldn't wring the guy's neck. Eric had been bad enough—

He stopped that thought cold.

"Gina." He cupped her shoulder. She leaned toward him, causing his heart to give a little lurch. The scent of a sun-warmed rose teased him. "Everything's ready for you."

"Mm."

He waited, then, "Do you need help getting ready for bed?"

Her eyes popped open. He smiled.

"I'm not—"

"—a child. Yes, I know." He did offer a hand up, however, as she swayed a little. "I found your nightgown. It's on the bed."

It was the longest ten minutes of his life, waiting for her. He hovered outside her door, listening for any indication she needed him, contemplating one of the items he'd found in her trunk—a sympathy card he'd sent after Eric's death. Inside it, his handwritten words, an offer of help, if she ever needed anything.

He didn't even remember sending it, but she'd kept it. No coincidence, after all. She'd been on her way to see him. *Why, Gina? What kind of trouble would make you come to me, a man you proclaimed to hate?*

Finally he heard the bed springs give a little and a murmur of sound from her.

"Everything all right?" he asked through the door.

"You can come in."

"Deputy seems to want to sleep with me," she said when he stepped into the room. "Is that okay?"

J.T. eyed the dog who was already curled up by her feet, a smug look in his eyes.

"He's a free agent," J.T. said, drawing a smile from her.

"Thank you for everything, Chief."

Chief. Well, that was one way of staying detached. "You're welcome. Good night, Gina."

She must've fallen asleep instantly. He padded around the room, hanging up her jacket, then putting her boots in the closet, needing order in the chaos of his mind. Finished, he leaned across her to pat the fickle dog good night, careful not to disturb her. She made a soft, sleepy sound.

"J.T.?"

His jolt of surprise came less from the fact she was awake but that it seemed both odd and familiar to hear her say his name.

"When I close my eyes, why do I picture you wearing a dark-blue uniform?"

Two

Gina felt him move away from the bed. Opening her eyes, she saw him silhouetted in the bathroom doorway, shoulders set and legs planted, poised for action. She took a moment to admire him, this duty-driven man. His leashed strength and unwavering focus were even more appreciated now that she and her precious cargo were snuggled in a warm bed, out of harm's way. It had been comforting hearing him move around the room, a brush of denim or a soft footfall the only sounds. But as she'd drifted toward sleep amid the peace his presence brought, a stark image of him imprinted itself in her mind.

"I thought you were asleep," he said, folding his arms across his chest.

She couldn't decide whether the edge in his voice was apology or accusation. "*Do* you wear a blue uniform?" she asked.

"No. Tan shirt, brown pants. Standard issue."

Her temple pulsed. She spun her wedding ring, still hoping to draw reassurance from it, still finding none.

"There's a photograph of me in a blue uniform with my parents in the hall outside the room," he said, "taken the day I graduated from the police academy. I spent nine years on the L.A.P.D. before I accepted this job."

She closed her eyes as fresh pain lanced her skull. Needing a diversion, she tried to focus on the conversation. "When did you move here?"

"What's wrong, Gina?"

Silent as a stalking panther, he'd returned to the side of her bed and crouched there, although he didn't touch her. She could've used a hug, a solid shoulder to lean on for just a minute.

"Do you need me to call Max? Are you in labor?"

Distract me, she begged him silently, wishing her head didn't hurt every time something threatened to cut through the barbed wire guarding her memory. "I'm all right. I realized I could use a couple of extra pillows, though, if you have some."

A cool breeze fanned her face at his instant departure. Deputy wriggled closer, then rested his head on her thigh, his liquid gaze uncensuring. The baby seemed settled, as well. Bracketed by baby and dog, Gina felt a contentment that she knew somehow was rare for her. Why?

And why wasn't her husband with her? Eric. He should love and protect—

Fear stuck its claws in her, its talons wickedly sharp. What if it was Eric she was running from?

What if it wasn't?

The chief suddenly loomed over her. "Are two pillows enough?"

She clenched the blanket with her fists, tucking it to her chin. Maybe she couldn't trust anyone, not even J.T. Ryker, chief of police of Lost and Found, California. And she was alone with him, under his complete control—

"Gina?"

Deputy lifted his head, whining a little. J.T. patted him, all the while observing something in Gina's expression he hadn't seen before. Had her memory returned? He stooped down until they were eye to eye. She drew back. The blanket she gripped like an iron shield shook.

"Don't be afraid of me," he said, guessing.

"I don't know you," she whispered, her eyes wide and searching.

"Yes, you do."

She shook her head.

"I'm the man who's going to protect you with his life."

A watery sheen coated her eyes. Her throat convulsed. "Why would you do that?"

Because I care about you. I always have. The words stayed locked tighter than a cell door. He had his orders from Max. He wasn't about to jeopardize her recovery by revealing they had a past, and a complicated one at that. Plus, she had a new man in her life, the father of the child she carried.

"I took an oath to protect and serve. It's not a promise I take lightly. You're safe with me, Gina. In every possible way."

She seemed to relax all at once. The blanket fluttered, then drifted over her body, molding it again. Her eyelids lowered a little, her mouth softened. Their gazes met and held. Then, amazingly, she cupped his face with her hand.

"I'll trust you," she said quietly.

"Good." He stood, breaking the contact. "I forgot to ask if you're hungry."

"Dr. Hunter gave me some soup while you were gone checking my car."

She reached for the extra pillows and pulled them under the blankets, one apparently to cushion her belly, the other she shoved farther down. Between her knees? Then she burrowed like a settling kitten.

"If you need anything at all, just shout. I won't be far," he said, clenching his fists. He never wanted to see that look of fear in her eyes again. "If Deputy becomes a pain in the rear, tell him to get out."

"Will he?" she asked, her voice slurred and sleepy. "Get out, that is?"

"Probably not. He's training impaired. But I'll hear and come get him."

She smiled, then her breathing took on the slow, easy rhythm of sleep.

J.T. left the bathroom light on and the door cracked open to guide her should she wake. He looked out the window of his bedroom, noted that the blizzard had let up. Still, between the snow and the televised Rose Parade and football games, people would likely stay home today, and he wouldn't be needed in his office. He'd heard the Caltrans crew pass by twice, already plowing the state highway. He lived close to the highway because of the accessibility, no matter what the weather. Most people would have to clear their own driveways or wait for Barney Cochran's teenage sons to roll out of bed and plow the private roads they were contracted to do. J.T. also needed to have Gina's car brought to his place.

His mouth twisted in a half smile. Everyone would see the unfamiliar car, and word would spread that he had a guest for the first time since he'd come to town. The rumors would start…

Turning from the window, he dropped onto his bed. With effort he tugged off his boots, then stretched out on the quilt, exhaustion rolling in waves down his body, but sleep not even a temptation. The nightmare would return. He didn't doubt it for a second.

How long could he stall it?

He drew a deep, settling breath. That didn't help, either. Gina's perfume clung to his shirt, reminding him of their first meeting. She, a Phoenix, Arizona, transplant about to start her sophomore year at the University of Southern California. He, a thirty-one-year-old big-city cop trying not to let the job make him too cynical.

He had taken the youth athletic league team he co-coached with his partner, Eric Banning, to Tony's Pizza after they'd won the age-ten-to-twelve division championship. Somewhere between the game and the party, Eric had disappeared—not a surprise. J.T. never had figured out why Eric had wanted to help coach, since he showed up only sporadically at the practices and games. He'd probably met some woman in the stands or the parking lot or at a traffic signal, and had gone off with her, his usual modus operandi. J.T. wasn't about to let it spoil the kids' celebration.

That first hot slice of pepperoni and sausage was calling his name when Gina walked through the door, wearing jeans, a plain white T-shirt, black leather jacket and boots, her long, dark hair shiny, her eyes sparkling. He barely noticed the two young women flanking her. Why would he? She was magnetic.

The restaurant might as well have been empty, except for them. Her eyes met his, and he finally understood that time really could stand still. Her smile froze, then softened before she looked away, her brows lifting at the last second, as if asking him a question she didn't want to wait to have answered.

One by one his young players left with their families. He stayed and watched as she shot some rounds of pool, her jeans cupping an enticing rear end, the rest of her just as curvy. Leaning against her propped cue stick between shots, she returned his stare, less blatant but just as frequent.

It was crazy. He didn't pick up women, yet he wanted to drive this one home and sleep with her that very night. Hell, he would've taken her right then and there on the pool table if he could have.

And because his attraction was so powerful, he waited for her to make the first move.

She finally did. After winning her fourth match, she silently held out a cue stick. Anticipation roared through him as he accepted her invitation. Or was it a challenge?

"J.T. Ryker," he said as he wrapped his hand around the stick, taking care not to touch her.

"I'm Gina Benedetto." She cocked her head. "And J.T. stands for…?"

A drift of flowery perfume reached him. "Jasper Thelonius."

Her eyes twinkled. She leaned into him a little, her radiant heat stoking his fire a little hotter. "Or perhaps Jarvis Thurgood?"

"One's as good as the other."

"I'll find out, you know. Somehow."

Because he was tempted to kiss the smile off her lips, he reached around her to pick up a cube of chalk, his arm brushing hers. The air popped and sizzled between them. *Out of control. This is way out of control.* Shaken, he took a step back, hiding behind the motion of chalking the cue tip. "May I buy you a beer, Gina Benedetto?"

"You could, um, Junior Titus—" she flirted easily, naturally "—but the cops would probably haul you in."

He knew, then. Knew before she said the words that there was no future with her, not tonight, not any night.

"I'm eighteen," she added. "Nineteen soon, though."

Eighteen. Might as well be a century between them. She hadn't lived yet. And he...he had already lived too long.

Not finding a robe among the clothes in her closet, Gina showered and dressed before she left the guest room at a little past noon. Her night's sleep had been interrupted several times by periodic trips to the bathroom or to walk off leg cramps. She might not be fully rested—was anyone this pregnant ever fully rested? she wondered—but she was relaxed. And hopeful.

No headache, so far. That was progress.

Her stomach rumbled, sending her in search of food. She wondered if the chief was at home. A glance into his bedroom as she'd shut and locked both bathroom doors had netted her a glimpse of an imposing four-poster bed. Sturdy pine furnishings and a cobalt-blue comforter and curtains lent a strong, masculine look to the tidy but warm and inviting room, one free of clutter or knickknacks. On the walls hung a couple of seascape watercolors that she wanted to inspect a little more closely, but she wouldn't enter his room without an invitation. He'd already helped her above and beyond his responsibilities as a police officer, without complaining about the imposition.

Gina admired his house as she moved from room to room. The comfortably rustic furnishings melded with trees and mountains visible through huge windows, creating an indoor environment as impressive as the outdoor one. This wasn't a house but a home, well loved and tended.

She found him sitting at a counter in the kitchen, sipping from a mug and reading, and dressed in his uniform, a gun holstered at his waist. He looked up from the book. Her breath caught a little at the intensity in his rich, golden eyes. Although his gaze never strayed from her face, she *felt* him look her up and down, as if she were a slender, sexy woman instead of…what she was. *Wishful thinking,* she chided herself, then frowned. She had no business wanting him to see her as a woman. She was married—

"Good morning," she said firmly, changing the direction of her thoughts. He didn't smile, exactly, but his expression wasn't as fierce as last night. He really was an attractive man, in an I'm-the-boss kind of way, his uniform reinforcing the all-male, in-charge impression. She didn't know a person could set his jaw that hard without shattering it.

"Sleep well?" he asked.

"Hmm." She craned her neck to see the title of the book: *Pregnancy and Childbirth.* "A little light reading?"

"Found it in your trunk. I've been trained in how to

deliver a baby, but I don't know much about pregnancy.'' He pointed to a cutaway drawing of an eight-months-pregnant woman. ''This is you right now. How do you breathe?''

''Breathing's not as much a problem as staying within bathroom range.'' She examined the picture a little more closely. ''I feel sorrier for the baby, all cramped up like that.''

This time his gaze did encompass her whole body, then lingered on her belly, as if he had permission now to look.

He picked up his mug again. ''So, does 'hmm' mean you did or didn't sleep well?''

''As well as can be expected.''

''You didn't ask for help.'' Accusation and maybe even disappointment rang in his words.

''I didn't need any. But thank you for the offer.'' She smiled at him, hoping to break the tension.

His frown deepened.

''Look, Chief, I've got enough problems without you being mad over whether I can find the bathroom during the night. If I couldn't take care of myself, I wouldn't have left home, I think, no matter what the situation there. Okay?''

He raised his hands in surrender. ''Are you hungry?''

''Starved.''

He started to stand. She put a hand on his shoulder to keep him in place, felt his muscles clench. ''I can fix something for myself. Have you eat— Oh! Good morning, baby.''

She closed her eyes a moment as she flattened her hand on top of her belly. ''She's been quiet this morning. I'd started to worry.''

"She?"

A smile lit up her eyes. "Don't ask me how I know that. Do you want to feel her?"

Before he could answer, she grabbed his hand and placed it where hers had been. Even though her sweater made a bulky barrier, the intimacy startled him silent. The wonder of feeling something poking at her from inside made him relax his hand.

"Amazing, isn't it?" she said, breathless, then laughed when the baby kicked harder.

J.T. stood. He couldn't allow that kind of bond to form between them, not now, not ever. That baby belonged to some other man.

And becoming a father was a fantasy J.T. had long ago abandoned.

"Max wants you to call him," he said abruptly, picking up the phone and punching a speed dial number. "I'll fix breakfast today. Tomorrow you can."

"You expect me to still be here?" She put the receiver to her ear. "No reports have come through?"

"None. Oatmeal okay?"

"Do you have chocolate chips?"

He must have looked at her as if she'd lost her mind, because she grinned.

"Cravings. It's like eating an oatmeal and chocolate chip cookie for break— Good morning, Dr. Hunter. This is Gina Banning."

J.T. listened to her answer Max's questions as he measured water, salt and oatmeal into a microwavable bowl, then went in search of chocolate chips. He'd already fixed a bowl of orange sections, mixed with banana slices and sprinkled with chopped walnuts. It had been a long time since he'd made anyone breakfast.

"He says my blood pressure was pretty high last

night, so he'll stop by in a little while to check it again,'' Gina said, coming up beside J.T. ''What can I do to help?''

''Everything's under control. No chocolate chips, but I can break up a candy bar, if that'll work.''

''That would be great. Just a few small pieces tossed in when the oatmeal is done. A little goes a long way. Thanks.'' She pressed her cheek to his arm for a second, then moved away.

Hell. He'd forgotten how touchy-feely she was. This was never going to work. She was only adding fuel to the explosion sure to blast the roof off when her memory returned—and she was bound to blame him. He would take responsibility for the other times she'd gotten mad at him, because he'd brought that upon himself, but not this time. Not for following orders. Well, maybe Max had finished his research on amnesia and would decide it was okay to give her some of her missing puzzle pieces. J.T. needed to know why she was here. He wanted to know why she was pregnant but not married.

''The coffee's decaf,'' he said, angling his head toward the coffeemaker. ''But there's milk and orange juice, too.''

She helped herself to the juice. ''Where's Deputy?''

''He's got a dog door, so he comes and goes.'' He started the microwave, then leaned against the counter, his arms and ankles crossed. ''I'm surprised he's stayed outside this long, actually, given how deep the snow is and how little he likes cold weather. He usually finds himself a sunny spot in the living room to nap in.''

''Your home is beautiful. And the view! The view is simply spectacular.''

''It was a big change for a city boy. Hadn't even

seen snow until I moved here. I had to learn how to drive in it.''

She swirled her juice in the glass, eyeing it instead of him. ''Is there enough social life here for you? I mean, I assume you're not married or I would've met Mrs. Ryker by now.''

''I keep her locked in the attic.''

Her head lifted in a flash. She frowned, then she tossed a paper clip at him.

He caught it on the fly. ''There's no Mrs. Ryker. It wouldn't be easy being married to me. I'm never really off duty, although I'm not always on the clock. I tend to stay in uniform, because looking the part is half the battle.''

''It suits you.''

Simple words accompanied by her slow, thorough inspection of his…uniform, he assumed. But the flicker of purely female interest he saw in her eyes whisked him back to the night they'd met.

After a few seconds she put a hand to her forehead. ''Headache again?'' he asked.

She nodded. ''That was sudden. I'd been doing so well, too.''

''Any other memories come to you?''

''Images that don't make sense.''

''Like what?''

She settled on a stool at the counter, set her glass down with a precise movement, then rolled it between her hands. He reminded himself that she didn't remember him, that even though she said she would trust him, they were only words, and certainly not reason enough for her to confide in him. Some amount of caution would be ingrained in her.

''It's as if someone took a bunch of movie clips and

put them onto one tape,'' she said after a while. ''Flashes of people, and all of them seemed...I don't know, angry or something.''

''At you?''

''I'm not sure. There's a man—he's young and nice looking. He isn't as tall as you, I don't think, and he's kind of stocky. Or maybe he's just muscular. It's hard to tell. His hair—'' she sliced a hand front to back over her head ''—is cut really short, like a soldier.''

Eric, J.T. thought.

''He's wearing a suit and tie, and there's a flower on his lapel, so maybe it's my wedding. Maybe he's my husband? Why wouldn't I recognize him, though? Then there's a woman, not my mother, but about her age, and she's crying. Crying so hard and pointing at me. And then the scene switches to my father, calling me...''

Pain dulled her voice, stealing what J.T. had always been drawn to—her optimism. She'd seen the good in everything, everyone...except him. She'd never forgiven him for what she called ''leading her on'' that first night, then turning his back on her.

''My father is calling me a brood mare. He's saying he thought I was smarter than that.''

The defeat in her posture knocked on J.T.'s teetering wall of detachment. ''Do you think these images are real or dreams?''

''I saw them as I woke up, so I hope they're dreams.''

The microwave beeped. He leaned across the counter and wrapped his hands around hers, still clamping the glass. ''Let it go for now, Gina.''

She lifted her gaze. ''But to run like I did, J.T.? I had to be protecting my baby. Nothing else makes sense. I think what hurts is that I don't seem to have anyone I trusted enough to help. Don't I have friends? Why wouldn't I go to my parents? Or one of my brothers or sisters? I have three of each, you know. Three older sisters and three younger brothers."

J.T. served her breakfast as she sat, her chin propped on her hand, a frown of concentration on her face.

"I grew up in Phoenix. Wouldn't I drive in that direction instead of north?"

"Too obvious a place to hide…if that's what you're doing."

"Lost and Found seems like a good place to hide." She dipped her spoon into the cereal. "How did you end up here?"

"Purely by chance." At least this much of the story he could tell her honestly. "After I left L.A. I decided to travel. A couple of months into the trip I stopped here and had lunch at Belle's Diner. By the time lunch was over, a bunch of the townspeople had held a meeting right there in front of me, then offered me the job of police chief, fire chief, dog catcher and anything else they thought of along the way, as necessary. They'd been looking for six months."

"And you said yes."

"I gave it some thought. About ten seconds." He smiled at the memory. "Aaron Taylor walked over to his hardware and auto parts store, and came back with a gold badge, Deputy, his food and water dishes, and a warning that the dog howled when left alone. He still does."

"Why did you leave L.A.?"

The back door opened, bringing a blast of cold air, nature's change of subject. Deputy charged into the adjoining utility room, followed by Max, who stomped his boots on a throw rug just inside the door.

"Sun's breaking through. It's blinding out there," he announced. "Your dog treed Mrs. Foley's cat again."

J.T. grimaced. "So that's where he's been." He walked past Max and grabbed his jacket from a peg by the door. "I'd better go rescue the cat before Mrs. Foley starts hollering. Think I'll swing by my office for a few minutes, too, if you don't mind."

Max followed him out the door. "You want me to baby-sit?"

"Does she need it?"

"It's probably not a good idea to leave her alone yet." Max lowered his voice. "From what I've learned, we were right to let her try to work things out on her own first. After a few days we might jog her memory along a little."

And so the charade continues, but at what cost? J.T. wondered.

The door opened behind them.

"Anything you have to say about me can be said *to* me," she told them, her fists propped on her hips. "In fact, I insist."

J.T. smiled at the sight. Did she really think she looked tough? Not with her hair swirling around her shoulders like that and her cheeks glowing pink. And especially not with those all-too-feminine curves. Tough? Nope. Soft and maternal. Irresistible.

Irresistible? He swallowed against the significance of the word.

"I'm serious," she said.

"Good thing I'm the one with the gun."

Her eyes narrowed. She started down the stairs. "Look, Chief—"

"Stay put. I'll explain," Max said, as the telephone rang inside the house.

"Mrs. Foley," J.T. muttered.

"I'll handle her, too."

"Handle?" Gina repeated, dangerously low.

"A figure of speech," Max said.

"It better be." J.T. gritted his teeth. He looked at Gina, wondering if she'd heard.

She stared at him, into him. The phone stopped ringing, leaving a stinging silence. He could try to back-pedal and end up looking more ridiculous than he already did, or he could ignore it, hoping she didn't read too much into his spontaneous remark.

What was that old saying? Better to keep your mouth shut and be thought a fool, than to open it and remove all doubt?

No doubt about it, he was a damned fool when it came to her. Always had been. Max didn't help, either, by just standing there, grinning like an idiot.

The moment stretched like cheese on pizza, a long string of awkwardness, getting thinner and thinner.

"Take your time. I'll be fine," Gina said, kindly slicing through the tension.

Well, Mark, what would you say about that? he asked his brother silently. The damsel rescues the knight. Chivalry's not dead. It's just switched genders.

Three

Except for the crackle and hiss from the fireplace, it was quiet. Gina eased into wakefulness, trying to recapture bits and pieces of a new dream, something to do with pool tables and pizza. The man with the military haircut was there, laughing, sliding his arm around her waist. J.T. stood nearby, somber and watchful, wearing a dark-blue uniform. Every time she walked toward him, he disappeared. The other man kissed her—

Her eyes flew open. Disoriented and breathless, she looked around J.T.'s living room, where she'd taken her third nap of the day. The lights were off except for one small table lamp. A glance at the mantel clock told her it was a little past ten o'clock. She'd slept for two hours straight—a record.

And she was safe. Her heart stopped thundering; tension melted away.

"I thought I heard you moving around."

J.T. came into view, a comforting sight.

"Then you must have incredible hearing," she said, admiring his long, lean lines for a moment. Pregnancy hadn't made her immune to him as a man. He'd been good company all day, besides. Not very talkative, but an attentive listener. "I haven't moved, Chief. I can't."

He crouched beside her, concern in his eyes. "What do you mean?"

"Your sofa is way too cushy. I think I'm embedded for life. Or until I get my abdominal muscles back."

He helped her to sit up, then sat beside her, his expression serious. The clock ticked. The fire popped. Remnants of the dream knotted her stomach. Still, she was intrigued by him. There had been moments since she'd dropped into his life that he seemed to wish he'd never been saddled with her. Other times he looked so deep into her that heat radiated head to toe at the invasion. She'd felt at ease with him almost from the beginning, but this was the first time he'd chosen to sit so close to her...

Oh. She understood now. His home and office computers were linked. He was about to give her news she wasn't going to like.

"Some chicken soup?" he asked.

"In a little while." She linked her fingers, squeezing until they hurt. Her imagination ran wild with possibilities. "What have you found out?"

His hesitation was tangible. "Nothing."

"Is that the truth?"

"You asked me not to feed your name into the system, but so far no one has reported you as missing."

"What do you think it means?"

Again a hesitation, this time a little more ominous.

"Frankly, I'd feel more comfortable if someone was searching for you through legal channels."

"Me, too." Pushing herself up, she walked to the fireplace and held her hands out to the flames. The heat barely penetrated her cold skin—and colder thoughts. "There's another possibility, though. Maybe no one cares that I'm gone. Which is worse, do you think?"

"Gina—"

"No. Please don't baby me. I need to know what I'm facing."

She heard him come up behind her. He didn't touch her, yet his warmth transferred to her. He would protect her with his life, he'd said. She believed him, and with that belief came trust, 100 percent.

She stared at her wedding ring. Pain hammered her head, vibrated behind her eyes. Instead of ignoring the signal and backing away from it, she tried to focus on what it meant.

"What if there's a reason that I don't feel married? Maybe I'm not. I might be wearing a ring so that people won't think the worst of me." She shook her head. "No. That wouldn't explain why Eric's name is on the health insurance card."

J.T. stood behind her, waiting for her to reach the next logical conclusion: that her husband wasn't alive. As soon as she figured that out, memories might come faster than she could cope with, but at least they would know why she was here and where the father of her child was.

And why that phantom man wasn't taking care of her.

"I can't think about it anymore. I need positive thoughts right now, for my baby's sake," she said with a note of finality. "Chicken soup, you said?"

"Or anything else you feel like eating." Anticipating her next move, he took a step back as she turned, her belly a whisper away from brushing his.

"Have I said thank you for all you're doing, Chief?"

"Not in the past two hours."

The phone rang. He grabbed the portable receiver he'd brought with him. "Chief Ryker."

"How's the patient?"

J.T. eyed her. She'd moved to look out the picture window and was staring at the cloudless night sky, her hands gliding in circles over her belly, as if massaging the baby. "You can ask her yourself, Max. She actually speaks English."

Over her shoulder she smiled at him. He passed her the phone then headed for the kitchen to heat up the soup. He'd already figured out that she was more comfortable eating a small meal every few hours, so he'd adjusted his schedule to her needs. It hadn't been difficult to cater to her, just a battle to get her to let him.

She came into the kitchen as he started the microwave.

"Max wants you to take my blood pressure, then for one of us to let him know what it is."

"Okay." He dug his keys out of his pocket. "I'll get my bag from the car."

"So, are you a paramedic besides being the chief of police?"

"No, but I've had advanced training. The nearest hospital is forty-five minutes away." He headed out the door.

"Where do you keep the saltines?"

"The doctor wouldn't approve."

"What's soup without crackers?" she grumbled.

"Easier on your blood pressure." The snow

crunched under his boots as he made his way to the car and scooped up his first aid bag. The cold penetrated his clothes, his skin, his muscles. He filled his lungs with frigid air, letting his mind clear. The attraction to Gina that had gut punched him years ago hadn't faded, except to add another dimension—her vulnerability, which tempted him way too much.

He could almost hear his brother chuckle. "Knights and damsels again, J.T.?" Mark would have said, sarcasm heavy in his voice. "You've become tiresome."

Was it chivalrous to care about a young woman who was married, almost died in a car accident, then was widowed, all within a three-month period? Or was it human decency?

She'd suffered. She'd grieved.

And she'd healed.

Or had she? She was different now, but that was to be expected. Three years had passed. Maturity came with experience. She'd fallen in love with someone else. Then again, maybe someone had taken advantage of her vulnerability after Eric's death, putting her in the predicament she was in now.

Some nameless, faceless rival had—

Rival? Hell.

He tramped back to the house, stomped off snow as he climbed the stairs. Warmth bathed his face as he stepped into the kitchen. Homey scents teased his nose. Deputy greeted him as if he'd been gone for hours instead of minutes. And Gina ladled soup into bowls.

The whole domestic scene irritated him. He wanted his peaceful life back. He wanted privacy again, to eat when he wanted, to sleep through the night, the only possible interruption being job related.

And he wanted her to stop smiling at him. She'd

peeled off her sweater in anticipation of having her blood pressure taken, he decided, and her turtleneck T-shirt clung to her body. He didn't think she'd gained a lot of weight, except in the obvious places.

"I guess I'm a lot of trouble, huh?" she asked as she pushed her sleeve above her elbow and sat on the stool.

Hell. She needed reassurance, and he wasn't in the mood to give it. He dug out his equipment from the bag. "You're no trouble."

"Which is a bald-faced lie. Somehow I'll make it up to you."

"You don't owe me anything." He wrapped the blood pressure cuff around her arm and tucked her hand alongside his body. Stethoscope in place, he pumped up the cuff. Then, instead of looking at the dial, he made the mistake of looking at her face first. Into her dark, smiling eyes, full of apology. At her gently curling lips, full of promise.

Her flowery scent jump-started a reaction that he quashed instantly. He couldn't think of her in that way. She was pregnant. Very pregnant. His only thought should be to protect her and her unborn child.

Yeah, right. So tell that to my—

Her blouse fluttered, as if the baby had kicked.

Damn it, Gina. You know how relentlessly cruel the world can be. Of all people, you should know better than to bring a child into it…

It wouldn't matter to her, he realized. She didn't see the same darkness he did, only a bright future with a baby she already loved. He wished he could recapture that long-lost innocence himself.

"Chief?"

He hadn't been paying attention. "I'm out of practice,'' he said, pumping up the cuff again. ''Sorry, but I've got to redo this.''

Her hand propped comfortably against his warm, hard body, Gina watched his frown deepen into a scowl. She couldn't imagine him being incompetent at anything, which meant that the news must be really bad, she decided. Her blood pressure was off the charts or something.

''One-sixty over a hundred,'' he said, sliding the cuff off her.

''But that's the same as this morning.''

''I know it's high as a reading, but is it high for someone pregnant?''

''Max would like to see it a little lower. Aside from thinking good thoughts, I don't know what I can do about it.''

''The same course of action as for anyone, I imagine. Avoid salt. Exercise. We'll go for a couple of walks tomorrow.''

Curious at his detachment, she pushed down her sleeve as he stowed his equipment.

Hours later she was still curious. Resting her back against the bed's headboard, she contemplated how he'd retreated from her. Maybe he'd finally reached the limits of his patience. Maybe it was a character flaw of hers—that she always tested someone's patience. Her head ached at the thought.

Meaning what? she wanted to shout. Ow. She rubbed her temples. Stupid headaches. Max seemed to think that the amnesia was more emotional than physical. She was hiding from something too painful to remember.

Think good thoughts, she reminded herself. Good thoughts. She imagined the sun setting into the ocean.

Gulls soaring. Surf pounding. Sand between her toes. A warm, tropical breeze blowing her hair from her face.

"Can't sleep?" Wearing sweatpants and a T-shirt, the chief was leaning a shoulder against the door frame, his arms folded over his chest.

She admired the purely masculine pose for a moment as she speculated on whether he usually slept in the nude. Her heart danced a quick tango at the wayward thought. Why didn't she feel faithful to someone? Loyal? Loving? Why was this man making her stomach flutter without any effort on his part whatsoever? What kind of woman was she, anyway?

"The baby has the hiccups," she said, ignoring the list of unanswerable questions. "Come feel."

He didn't move.

"Pregnancy tends to obliterate modesty, Chief. People touch my tummy all the time."

He'd mastered the silent debate, she decided, trying not to smile. It had taken her a while, but she'd finally coaxed him out of his bad mood earlier by pretending to add salt to her soup. He just needed a little more coaxing. "We won't bite."

Low light from the bathroom cast him in a rugged silhouette as he came toward her and sat on the edge of the bed. Deputy lifted his head, then curled into a tighter circle, ignoring them.

"Use both hands," she told the chief, pushing the blankets past her abdomen. "Her whole body jumps."

After a slight pause, he settled his hands on her, startling her into a new kind of awareness—only one layer of flannel lay between his hands and her skin. Her pulse escalated in tempo and volume. She tipped her head back into the pile of pillows fluffed behind her, taking a quick mental trip back to her peaceful beach. It felt good having his hands on her. Too good. Comforting…and much, much more.

"I'm going to miss touching her whenever I want," she said. "I love lying in the bathtub and watching her move around inside me."

"You can see her?"

"She does a little ballet in there." She moved his hands higher on her belly, enjoying how he smiled every time the baby hiccuped. "That's her bottom. Feel?"

He nodded.

She pressed his palms tight against her body, sliding one to each side. "These bumps are her elbows, I think."

"It's not smooth, like I thought it would be. You're actually kind of lumpy."

"Sometimes I'm even lopsided. The head's aimed down all the time now. Every once in a while it feels like her feet are hooked on my ribs."

"Does that hurt?"

"Sometimes."

J.T. broke contact with her, retreating from the intimacy, irritated with himself. Pregnancy was supposed to be a spiritual experience, yet his need for her was just as strong as the first time he'd seen her.

He tugged the bedcoverings over her. "How did you know that people touch your abdomen?"

She stopped smoothing the blankets. When she met his gaze, she frowned. "I can't picture anyone specific doing it, but why else would I feel so comfortable letting you?"

Because deep down you remember me. The thought scared him as much as it satisfied.

She yawned and stretched, then snuggled into the pillows.

"Have you slept at all?" he asked.

"Mmm-hmm. Did you?"

He nodded. He'd slept. Dreamed. Awakened in a cold sweat. The old, all-too-frequent nightmare that he'd finally laid to rest had clawed its way past the barrier he'd erected, the colors brighter, the ache exposed and raw. He resented her for waking the sleeping monster, exposing its fangs.

"Thanks for checking on me, Chief," she said, her voice husky with impending sleep. "But you don't have to keep me company."

"You probably wouldn't tell me if you needed anything, but I'm asking, anyway."

A second or two passed. "I'm fine, thank you."

He didn't miss her hesitation. From worry? Or fear, maybe? Her recent past was a blank, her future unknown.

And she didn't have anyone to lean on.

Well, he had broad enough shoulders—and a more-than-passing interest in her well-being. He wrapped a hand around one of hers. Her eyes widened. She went perfectly still. "What can I do for you, Gina?"

"I would love a back rub."

So much for his silent hope that her heart's desire was a mug of hot chocolate. "Get comfortable."

She situated pillows in a rustle of movement, until she was lying mostly on her side, the blankets bunched at her waist. Her long-sleeved, high-necked nightgown made no blatant invitation, but the fabric was soft, he discovered when he kneeled behind her and curved his hands over her shoulders, and her body was warm. Her sigh of appreciation sent Deputy's tail thumping slowly, heavily, as if he was the one getting the treatment. J.T. smiled at the dog, who'd abandoned his bed without a look back in order to sleep with Gina again.

When J.T. kneaded her shoulders, she moaned.

"Sorry," she said quickly.

"Don't apologize." He was relieved to discover she wore a bra, although the ridges of her backbone teased his fingertips, and the blunted curve of her shoulder blades grazed his palms. "What hurts?"

"Everything," she said, humor punctuating the word. "The weight in front constantly drags on the muscles in back. I can't tell you how good this feels."

Buried under the guilty pleasure of touching her lurked a stronger sense of rightness. Of destiny. Of lost opportunities. He wouldn't forfeit this one, as he had before.

"I hope you plan to go back to your normal routine tomorrow," she said, arching her back a little as he dragged his fingers down her spine, stopping just above her waist, then gliding up to her shoulders again.

"I'll do what needs doing."

"Can I go along with you?"

"You want to?"

"I don't figure you'll be agreeable to leaving me here by myself, Chief."

"The way I see it, people will be wanting to see who belongs to the car parked in my driveway."

Gina smiled into the pillow. "I've never lived in a small town. It's really different, isn't it?"

"Why don't you just go to sleep, Gina?"

"Because I'd miss enjoying the back rub."

"I'll give you a rain check for tomorrow."

"Really?" Some instinct told her that no one had

pampered her like this. "I sure got lost in the right town, didn't I?"

"Sleep."

Obedient, she drifted aimlessly toward slumber. His broad palms and strong fingers found every kink and knot, easing the soreness away. She almost purred as he threaded his hands through her hair to massage her scalp. After a while he gently pulled her hair away from her face, then the bed dipped under her as he climbed off it. The blankets settled over her like a cocoon.

Mmm. Thank you, she thought, unable to form words.

She felt his breath against her cheek, the brush of his lips to her hair. Oh! He was tucking her in.

She opened her eyes.

"You're supposed to be asleep," he said as he crouched beside the bed, a hint of irritation in his voice.

Or was it embarrassment?

"I don't think anyone has ever taken care of me the way you have." She swallowed against the sting in her throat.

"Maybe because you announce to the world how independent you are."

"I'm too defensive, aren't I?"

"There's probably a reason."

Urges she couldn't remember having before welled up inside her, primitive and earthy. He'd taken care of her, protected her, sheltered her. Made her feel like a desirable woman, yet without a hint of impropriety.

"I feel like I've known you forever," she said, her wedding ring burning like a branding iron.

"It's been a longer-than-average twenty-four hours because we haven't slept for eight of it."

"Something tells me that was more than just a logical observation."

He stood and headed toward the door. "Go…to…sleep."

"Yes, sir."

He flashed a look over his shoulder.

"What does J.T. stand for?" she called just before he got out of sight.

"Jasper Thelonius."

A flash of white light blinded her. A hammer struck an anvil inside her head, bam, bam, *bam.* She gulped for air. Breathe. *Breathe.* Visions came fast and furiously, like her dreams, not making sense. J.T., watching her, not smiling, hardly moving. The smell of pizza.

Pizza?

A pool table. The clack of balls.

Nauseated, she pushed herself up, grasped the bedside table, knocked the clock to the floor.

Footsteps pounded. The overhead light came on. The man in her vision, real now, fell to his knees beside her, calling her name.

"Why do I keep seeing you?" she asked, confused.

"What do you mean?"

"Like flashbacks. But they can't be flashbacks, can they, because I keep seeing *you.* And I smell pizza. There's a pool table. I don't understand." She moaned. "My head hurts so much."

"I'll call Max."

"I think I'm going to be sick."

Amid her protests, he scooped her into his arms, delicately, not jarring her in the least. The moment he set her down in the bathroom, she gasped.

Plucking at her nightgown, she stared at the floor. "I think my water just broke."

Four

While Max examined her, J.T. paced outside her bedroom door. She'd started having contractions sometime between her water breaking and Max's arrival a half hour later. So much for thinking they had a few weeks' leeway.

The door opened. Max peered out. "You can come in."

J.T. assessed her. Wide-eyed but calm. She even smiled at him.

"You've got options, Gina," Max said, including J.T. in the conversation with a gesture. "You can go to the hospital, of course. I'll go with you and deliver the baby, if you want. Or we could set up at my clinic. My equipment is state-of-the-art. Or you can stay here, and I'll bring the necessary equipment to you."

"It's safe for me to have a home birth?" Gina asked. "The baby's early."

"Not too early."

"J.T.?"

Moving closer to the bed, he answered the question he saw in her eyes. "Whatever you want is fine with me."

"I want to stay here."

Max nodded. "J.T., give Rosie a call. See if she'll meet me at the office in fifteen minutes. Rosie's my assistant," Max said to Gina. "She has four kids of her own. You'll be glad she's here."

Hours passed. The sun rose. Her contractions got closer and stronger. Feeling helpless, J.T. hurt every time she did. The atmosphere of the bedroom was an odd combination of clinical and casual. Max and Rosie played gin rummy while keeping an eye on the fetal monitor. Sometimes they unhooked her, and Gina walked the house, hoping to speed things up. J.T. made himself scarce each time Max examined her, but couldn't wait to get back to her, fresh ice chips in hand, grateful she'd seemed to forget the "flashbacks" she'd had before her water broke.

They rarely spoke. He rubbed her back, gave her an arm to lean on when she walked and a clean pair of his socks when her feet turned icy. She drew his hand to her abdomen during contractions, amazing him with how hard it got, mumbling something about going to the beach as she breathed deeply, then drew a final cleansing breath at the end of the contraction.

Considering she hadn't started with a night's sleep, she had to be exhausted, but remained steadfastly cheerful. Rosie, the voice of experience, offered comfort in ways that neither Max nor J.T. could, advising her matter-of-factly about the process, tempering the information with humor and adding the phrase, "But it gets better eventually."

At about noon Max told her she could start pushing with the next contraction. She moved to the end of the bed, propped her feet on chairs.

"This'll work best if we can get you almost upright," Max said. "J.T., get behind her and support her back as she bears down."

Grateful for a job to do, he became her wall. Her back curved into his chest, her head rested against his shoulder. He pushed with her, holding his breath. Rosie urged her to push harder. Max saw the baby's head.

Gina rested after the contraction, melting against J.T., grateful for his unfaltering strength. "I can't believe I'm going to forget how much this hurts," she said to Rosie, who watched the fetal monitor.

"Nature's way of guaranteeing the future. I did it four times, didn't I? It may be the most painful experience of your life, but it's productive. Here we go again."

A memory of red-hot agony flashed in Gina's mind, hurting more than the rising contraction. "It's *not* the most painful—"

"Don't talk, honey. Take a deep breath and bear down."

"Doin' great, Gina," Max said. "This baby's got your head of hair."

J.T. said something, the words garbled, the tone encouraging. Nothing penetrated the horror she'd been swept into, a tornado of memories. A car slamming into another. Metal against metal. Shattering glass. Her body, broken and battered. Oh, the pain. The excruciating pain. A glimpse of Eric, bloody, unmoving.

Eric! Don't leave me!

"Gina, stop pushing. Stop."

Max, right in her face. J.T.'s arms tightening around her.

J.T.

He knew. He knew who she was. And he didn't tell her.

"What's happening?" J.T., something in his voice. Fear? Panic?

"Gina," Max said, soothing. "What's going on?"

"I remember. Oh, God. I remember."

"Contraction." Rosie, brisk, no-nonsense.

"You've got to bear down," Max ordered her. "Pay attention, Gina. Your baby needs you. Talk to her, J.T."

"Gina—"

"Don't!" She couldn't hold a breath to push. "You lied to me. Lied."

"Too late," Rosie said. "Pant, honey. Let's just get you through this one, then we'll start over."

"I don't want you to touch me, *Chief.* Defender of the *truth.* There's a joke." Gina spat the words over her shoulder. She saw the men communicate without speech, which infuriated her.

Max stood, leaned toward her. "J.T. wanted to tell you, but I wouldn't let him. Save your anger for after the baby is here—and direct it at me. Now, let's get back to business here."

"Away we go," Rosie said. "Time to work."

Tears collided with sweat on Gina's face. She pushed as hard as she could, channeling raw emotions, reliving the past. The comfort she'd found in having J.T.'s arms around her vanished. His strength meant nothing anymore. He'd interfered once before. Hurt her twice before. What right did he have to be there?

No. She wasn't being fair. She'd come to him intentionally, purposefully.

"Head's through. One or two more pushes, Gina. Hang in there."

She didn't speak. Couldn't speak. Barely listened, even, except to her body and its demands. She groaned, grunted, pushed. Then the next time the shoulders were through.

"A boy," Max said, setting the squalling infant on her abdomen.

"Boy?" Why had she been so sure it was a girl? Hesitant, she looked at the baby. A boy. Ten toes and fingers. Flailing arms and legs. It was true. Relief made her dizzy. Her heart thudded, her eyes burned. It was worth it—everything she'd been through. All the pain, all the worrying. Worth it. All these months, intentionally not finding out whether it was a boy or a girl, because she had no control over it and she wanted to enjoy the pregnancy, no matter what.

But it was a boy.

Thank you, God. My job is done.

"Need you to push one more time, Gina."

The placenta, she realized, pushing with less force, then going limp. J.T.'s arms were still around her, but he said nothing. She didn't care anymore. She'd survived the accident, and now she had fulfilled her promise.

A son. An end and a beginning, she thought, dazed. A gift, one that freed her of the past and opened up a brand-new future.

Through a haze of exhaustion Gina watched Max cut the cord, snipping the physical connection. Her son was his own person now, dependent on her, but individual. In fulfilling her obligation, she'd also placed a burden on him for the future, and his own sense of duty. She would tell him how he came to be, what made him so special.

Rosie took over. She'd brought a baby bathtub with her, and efficiently cleaned him. He stopped crying.

"Is he okay?" Gina asked, the quiet seeming ominous.

"He's just fine, aren't you, sweet pea?" Rosie crooned. "Chief, you can let mama lie down now."

J.T. slipped out from behind her, then jammed pillows under her shoulders and head. He had no idea what he was supposed to do, but he figured she would want time alone with her son—and her restored memory.

Whoever the father of her child was, *he* would be on her mind now—rightfully so. Their moment out of time was gone. Even though Max took the blame for not telling her the truth, she would still be angry at J.T. He knew that. Accepted that.

But he'd done his duty by her. She'd counted on him, and he hadn't failed her.

"What's his name, honey?" Rosie asked.

"Joel Eric Banning," Gina said with a catch in her voice. "After his father. We'll call him Joey, I think."

J.T. looked at Max, who stopped what he was doing long enough to frown in return. The long, hard delivery had done something to her mind, J.T. thought. Whatever memories had surfaced during delivery were distorted, manifestations of the dreams she'd told him about, not the truth.

"I wish you and Max would stop talking to each other with your eyes," Gina snapped. "I haven't lost my mind. Eric *is* his father. And yes I know he's been dead for more than three years."

She had to look over her shoulder at him, since he was standing back, not wanting to see what Max was doing to her down...there. He and Rosie went about their business as if nothing was happening, no discussion taking place.

"You were his partner, J.T. Didn't you know how important having a son was to him?"

"We never talked about it. Even so, how could he be the father?"

"Haven't you ever heard of sperm banks?"

Eric's child? Not some other man's? Not someone else she'd loved and trusted?

Then what was she running from?

Rosie put the baby in J.T.'s arms. "Hang on to him for a few minutes, will you, while we get mama cleaned up. You might want to wait outside."

He stared at the bundle squirming in slow motion in his arms. A tiny mouth opened and closed, a little pink tongue poking out. His face reddened, as if he was gathering enough steam to howl.

"Can I see him first?" Gina asked, sounding anxious.

The quicksilver change in her set a whole new tone, wiping out any lingering anger. Everyone seemed to relax at the same time. There would be time for questions later, when she'd rested. When they were alone. For now, she was a new mother, with a strong need to assume her role.

J.T. transferred him awkwardly to the crook of her arm. Then just as he started to step back, Joel Eric Banning—the son of the man J.T. despised—opened his eyes and looked directly at him. *Don't do this. Don't make me care.* J.T.'s silent plea came too late.

It had taken only the one look, one filled with helplessness and innocence.

"He's beautiful, isn't he?" Gina asked, glowing. Her hair had come loose from the band. The strain of giving birth showed on her face. Sweat-dampened hair clung to her cheeks and neck. But the Gina he'd cared about for so long was there, too, her dark eyes shining, her smile gentle. Maternal, maybe. Because he couldn't stop himself, he kissed her forehead, brushing her hair back from her face at the same time.

"I thought you hated me," he whispered so that only she could hear.

"Maybe for a little while. But not now."

"Why are you here?"

She touched his cheek, a whisper of a caress. "I needed you."

Sweet words. "Gina—"

"You two can talk later," Rosie said, shooing him away. "Take the boy for a walk around the house for a few minutes, J.T. I'll let you know when to come back."

He lifted the baby. "He'll be fine," he assured Gina.

She smiled back. "I know."

J.T. headed for the door.

"You know you're B-negative, Gina?" Max asked.

"Yes. Eric was A-positive."

"If the baby's positive, you'll need a shot of Rh-immune globulin."

"No, I'm all set. I had it after my first pregnancy."

The doorknob slipped from J.T.'s hand. He walked away, her child in his arms, his mind a whirling pinball machine flashing TILT in red neon, his legs moving only by sheer will.

My first pregnancy.

He could understand her forgetting Eric for a while, considering the trauma of the accident. But a child? How the hell had she forgotten a child?

At midnight Gina leaned over the bassinet that Rosie had brought, listening to her son breathe. Bundled like a mummy, Joey slept. With Rosie's guidance she'd nursed him a few times, although her milk wouldn't come in for a day or more. After some prodding, he'd latched on with gusto, startling a laugh out of Gina and gaining a nod of satisfaction from Rosie. "Excellent," she'd said. "He'll get a good dose of colostrum. It'll keep him healthy."

Healthy. That's all Gina wanted. Good health. Happiness. Peace.

At some point she would have to make the phone call she dreaded most. But not yet.

Gina heard J.T.'s car pull up. He'd responded to a call for a chimney fire a few hours ago, had left with an apology on his lips but with the rest of his body language announcing he was glad to get away. She'd been grateful, as well, needing some time alone, a luxury long denied her. Plus, he'd been distant all day. Oh, he was attentive in that he took care of her needs, but uncommunicative.

Her fault, she knew. There was a lot he didn't understand. And a lot that she didn't, either, including what had happened the first night they'd met—and the last.

Tightening the sash on the robe Rosie lent her, Gina shuffled down the hall and into the kitchen just as he opened the back door and stepped into the utility room. Deputy sped past her to greet him. Soot covered his face and hands. He must have left his firefighting gear outside to air. His hair was tousled, his feet covered by thick socks. She could only imagine how tired he was.

"What are you doing up?" he asked, moving to the sink and turning on the water. "I thought you'd be dead to the world by now."

"I was. Joey woke up, so I nursed him again. What happened at the fire?"

"Lots of smoke damage. Some water damage, too, but we saved the house. Everyone'll pitch in to help clean it up tomorrow."

She leaned her forearms on the counter. "I didn't know that kind of community existed anymore."

"Probably more than you think. Did Rosie leave?"

"I told her I'd be fine. She needed to get home to her family."

He pulled his T-shirt over his head, tossed it in the vicinity of the washing machine in the utility room, then soaped up his arms.

Gina swallowed. Even covered with grime he tempted. She remembered the first night at the pizza parlor—how his eyes had never left her alone for a second. It had been foolhardy, acknowledging an attraction to a stranger, yet she'd sensed more in him than a physical pull. Her imagination, of course. He'd shut himself off from her after exchanging only a few sentences. She never had figured out what she'd done to turn him off like that. Eric had arrived moments later, apologizing to J.T. for being late for some celebration, then zeroing in on her and, unlike J.T., not giving up. A month later they were married. She'd made him a promise—

"Baby's okay?" J.T. asked, reaching for a paper towel. She blinked. Focused. "He's fine."

"You?"

"All things considered, I'm doing okay. Just don't ask me to sit down."

He propped his hip against the counter and dragged the damp paper towel over his face, then down his chest. "You're quiet."

"You haven't smiled at me all day." She hadn't meant to sound pathetic, but it had come out that way.

"That matters to you?"

"I thought we were friends."

His silence escalated the tension. "Did you?" His eyes turned cold. "Friend to friend, would you like to tell me about your other child?"

Her eyes burned. Big mistake, she realized. She was in no condition to deal with anything emotional. She turned and walked away. "I promise I'll be out of your hair as soon as I can manage it. Good night."

She heard him swear. A single word. Succinct. Direct. If she were a swearing woman, she might have said the same thing about fifty times in a row. But she wasn't. She was a brand-new mother with raging hormones, a jelly belly, and an incredibly sore...nether region, as her mother would call it.

Tears spilled then. *I want my mother!*

"Gina." J.T. wrapped a hand around her arm, slowing her down, furious at himself. What kind of jerk was he, anyway, treating her like that? Okay, so he had some issues with her, questions for her, even some accusations he wanted to level. It was no excuse for making her cry.

"Just leave me alone."

"I'm sorry."

"No, you're not. You've always judged me and found me wanting. I've never known why." Her voice shook. She wiped a hand across one cheek, then the other. "And I don't have another child. I was pregnant when the car— When Eric— My injuries were too severe. I lost the baby."

Calling himself every name in the book, he reached for her. She jerked away. "I didn't know, Gina."

"We had just found out." She started to sob, big, shoulder-shaking sounds from deep, deep inside. "I didn't even get to feel my baby move."

He pulled her in his arms, holding tight when she fought him at first, then wrapping her closer when she gave in, her arms curving up his back, fingernails pressing into his flesh. He'd never heard anyone cry like that. Scorching hot tears washed his chest. He buried his face in her hair, breathed the fragrance so distinctly Gina, indulging a long-held fantasy he'd expected to go unfulfilled in his lifetime. It undoubtedly wouldn't happen again—he didn't count on her forgiving him.

"I'm sorry," he said again.

After a while she shuddered, her cheek still pressed against his collarbone, her arms still locked around him. "I'm a mess," she said.

"I don't know what it is about you that makes me act like an ass, Gina. But I always do. I'll try not to jump to conclusions anymore."

"It's okay," she said wearily. "You're confused. So am I. It's been a hard few days."

"Sounds like it's been a hard few years."

"That, too. But things are looking up." She stepped back, wiping her eyes. Cupping her elbow, he walked her into the bathroom, then ran cool water over a washcloth and handed it to her.

"Better," she said, straightening her shoulders, tossing back her hair, looking more like her old self. "You smell smoky."

"I'm going to get in the shower in a second."

"I need to use the bathroom first."

"No problem." He stepped past her.

"Thanks for being there today, Chief. For all you've done. I can't ever repay you."

He turned around. "Chief?"

"Oh. Sorry." A smile flickered across her lips. "I meant Jasper Thelonius."

He grunted. "Stick with Chief."

"Are you ever going to tell me what J.T. stands for?"

He moved close to her. Too close for comfort, he supposed. But those big brown eyes teased, and his memory played a few games of its own. He bent toward her. She went still. Her eyes searched his. All traces of humor fled. Their gazes locked, he brushed his lips across hers. Her eyes fluttered closed. Clenching his fists, he forced himself to walk away.

"Well," he heard her say. "I guess it means Just Teasing."

Five

By the time Gina ventured out of the bedroom with the baby the next morning, a rocking chair had appeared in the living room, placed where she could rock Joey and enjoy the majestic view of snow-covered trees and the Sierra Nevada mountains. She ran her hand along the intricately carved wood back. Someone had put their heart and soul into creating the fine piece of furniture.

"Good morning." Rosie bustled into the room, a dish towel thrown over her shoulder. The flyaway red hair she'd tamed into a ponytail yesterday made a kinky frame for her freckled face.

"Do I have you to thank for the rocking chair?" Gina asked, sitting gingerly.

"That would be the chief. I brought the cushion, though. A doughnut. You'll thank me." Her expression reflected sympathy in response to Gina's wince. "It'll get better eventually."

"They're going to carve those words into your tombstone."

"When you've got four teenagers, it becomes your mantra."

Gina studied her one-day-old son, who was fed and dry but awake. She knew he couldn't see clearly yet, but he seemed to focus on her when she talked, a little frown of concentration on his face. "I'm glad I've got a long time to wait."

"Sixteen years from now you'll be wondering where the time went. Well, what's first on your wish list— breakfast or a shower?"

"Oh! I would love a shower. I didn't realize that giving birth was so...so—"

"The technical term is 'yucky.' Wait'll your milk comes in."

Gina accepted Rosie's help to stand, then they headed toward the bathroom. "You must be curious about me. My situation."

"Honey, there's something you need to know about Lost and Found. Like all small towns, everyone knows everyone's business *now,* but not from before they got here. A lot of people come to start over. We don't ask questions. Some people stay. Some decide it's time to move on."

"Really? You have no past?"

"Not unless you want one. No one'll ask."

But the rule wouldn't apply to her, Gina realized. J.T. had a right to ask questions, a right to the truth. "Can I ask where J.T. is?"

"Doing his rounds. He makes a sweep through town a couple times a day, drives up and down every road, checks out every property.'' Rosie picked up the bassinet and carried it into the bathroom. ''He's been a good chief. The best we've had. Everybody respects him, even the ones he's arrested. He's got a way about him.''

Pride warmed Gina, even though his being a good chief had nothing to do with her. ''I'm surprised he hasn't married.''

Rosie gestured for Gina to put the baby in the bassinet, then she opened the shower door and turned on the water, testing it with her hand, adjusting the temperature. Apparently satisfied, she shut the door, trapping the steam. ''Now, see, Gina, that would be considered asking a question, even though there's no question mark at the end of the sentence.''

''I only meant that he's a good catch.''

''Plenty of folks would agree with you.''

''Plenty of women folk?''

''Men don't generally concern themselves with that particular issue.''

''Darn it, Rosie. I'm asking if he has a girlfriend.''

Rosie pursed her lips, which Gina thought could mean that she didn't like the woman, or that she was hesitant about answering.

''I don't rightly know if you can call her that,'' Rosie said finally. ''But there's someone he sees.''

A somersault of jealousy spiraled slowly into disappointment. So, the whisper of a kiss last night meant nothing. The caring, the concern, the tender treatment? Human decency. Obligation.

I thought you hated me, he'd said, with good reason. Yet it hadn't stopped him from being kind and generous to her. She wasn't even sure herself what she wanted from him, but the possibilities just got a lot more limited.

She stepped into the shower a minute later, grateful for the knowledge Rosie had armed her with, and blaming the ache inside on postpartum blues.

Above the noise of a hair dryer, J.T. heard female laughter, an unfamiliar sound in his quiet house. Deputy cocked his head at J.T., as if to say, "Somebody's having fun!"

"You like having company, don't you, boy?"

The dog barked once, his tail swinging hard enough to jerk his rear end from side to side. J.T. didn't for a minute believe Deputy was waiting for permission to join the women—*well trained* were not words anyone ever associated with the mutt—but he told the dog to go on, anyway.

J.T. lingered in the living room, wanting to be part of the fun, too, but knowing that the laughter would probably stop when Gina realized he was home.

He set the rocking chair in motion. Hell, he knew he was too serious, too literal. Enough people had told him so, but he figured it was part of what made him a good cop. What was wrong with that? When had *steady* and *reliable* become interchangeable with *boring?*

He blew out a breath. Other people's opinions weren't the issue at the moment. What ate at him now was the ten minutes he'd spent with Brynne Mc-Masters, a happy-to-be-single woman who, until now, had satisfied his occasional need for female companionship without complicating his life. He admired Brynne, a defiantly independent woman in her late twenties, with a rich laugh and a physical need that matched his, but her past was a closed subject, her source of income not apparent. Every once in a while they shared a steak, a bottle of chardonnay, some conversation and a tumble in bed.

She never asked for more.

He didn't have more to give.

Her house was the last stop on his rounds. Her A-frame cabin was situated about as far from town as she could get, tucked into a small forest. He'd surprised her today by asking to come in, startled her when he'd backed her against a wall as if he was going to take her there and then.

"I don't substitute," she'd said, her gaze direct.

Well, how damn low could he stoop, anyway? He stepped away from her. "I apologize. You didn't deserve that. I don't know what came over me."

"Some woman who's turned your civilized life upside down, I would guess. This isn't like you." She eyed him speculatively. "Or maybe it is, J.T. Did you think of that?"

He shoved his hands through his hair. "Hell, Brynne, she's too young for me."

"How young?"

"Twenty-two. I'll be thirty-five in a month. Not to mention, she gave birth to another man's child yesterday."

"That would seem to complicate matters."

The understatement had calmed him. He realized that if he had something to say, it should be to Gina. Problem was, he didn't know what.

He'd left Brynne on friendly terms. They both knew that the relationship was over, no matter what happened with Gina. They'd stepped into personal territory; too much would change because of that.

"Hey, J.T.," Rosie said, coming into the living

room. "I'm gonna fix mama some breakfast. Have you eaten?"

"You don't need to wait on me."

"I don't mind. You can keep Gina company while I'm fixing it. She just took a shower, and the poor thing's tuckered out. Needs to sit a spell."

Gina came through the doorway and headed to the rocking chair, her steps a slow shuffle. "Good morning."

"How're you feeling?" Judging by how carefully she sat, he could guess her answer.

"Rosie helped me shower. I can't remember one feeling so good before." She stroked the chair arms, curved her fingers over the polished ends. "This is a beautiful rocker."

Even her voice shook with exhaustion. J.T. made himself relax. Picking up an ottoman, he set it near her chair to sit on. "I borrowed it from Bear Ramierez. He makes furniture."

"He makes art," she said, patting the arms.

J.T. smiled. "I'll tell him you said so." He glanced toward the bedrooms. "Baby asleep?"

She nodded, her hair falling softly over her shoulders, a thick, shiny curl resting on each breast. She still had a tummy, and her eyes broadcast the toll of giving birth, but she looked beautiful. Not ethereal, but all too earthbound and real, if a little pale.

"Max said he'll stop by later. I'm supposed to call and tell him when you think you'll be napping."

"As soon as I've eaten. I know you have questions for me, too. I promise we'll talk tonight." She seemed to doze then.

The baby let out a wobbly cry. Deputy charged into the room and whined, like the town crier.

"I'll get him for you," J.T. said, seeing her exhaustion. "Before I do, though, I need to ask you one question."

Her eyes clouded. "Okay."

"Why did you leave home in such a hurry? Is there someone on your trail?"

She looked away from him. For a few long moments she stared out the window. "The snow's melting."

He waited. Joey's cries became more insistent. Deputy barked, then ran out of the room.

"Yes, someone's on my trail," she said finally. "Winnie Banning. My mother-in-law."

Gina welcomed nightfall, not because she would unburden herself to J.T., but because he was different at night, more mellow, more understanding. Or maybe it was because she couldn't see his face as clearly, couldn't read anything into his expression. Nighttime softened his edges.

She'd catnapped off and on all day. Max came and went. J.T. had helped clean up the fire-damaged house, made a late-afternoon check of the town, then had come home, quieter than usual. Rosie set dinner on the table, imparted a few final words of wisdom about the value of strategically placed ice packs, and returned to her own family.

The sound of J.T. showering comforted Gina now as she nursed the baby, making her feel that she had a family, a home—something she hungered for.

It wasn't her home, though. For one thing, at home she wouldn't have to worry about staying covered up while she nursed. It was hard enough getting the knack of it without fiddling with a blanket, keeping it draped over her. She ended up not able to watch Joey to make sure he was doing okay.

She could ask to have the rocking chair moved into the bedroom, of course, but then she would feel too isolated. She smiled. Apparently, there was just no pleasing her.

At the moment, however, there was no danger of J.T. walking in on her, not as long as she could hear the water running. So she left the extra blanket on her lap and enjoyed watching Joey nurse, his little fists tucked under his chin, pressing into her breast. Such a tiny thing, with such great power over her already.

"We're heart tied, sweetheart," she said softly. He drew a gulping little breath, and had to root for the nipple again. She guided him until he latched on, then she smiled at how much energy he gave to his task. "Do you know how long I waited for you? How long I've loved you? We're going to have a good life, you and me. A good life. What a gift you are, Joey. A miracle."

Wrapping him in a quilt of unconditional love, she stroked his hair, dark like hers, but silky soft. When he started fussing, she shifted him to the other side, leaving herself exposed to the air, as Rosie recommended.

The shower stopped running. She pictured J.T. drying off, wrapping a towel around his hips and coming to check on them. She saw him crouch in front of them, smile at them, as if they belonged to him. Impossible dreams.

Reality returned a few minutes later when he did come into the room, dressed in sweatpants and a T-shirt. He didn't even glance their direction—his way of giving her privacy, she supposed—but headed to the fireplace and stirred up the logs, adding one. He stayed crouched in front of the hearth, which gave her time to appreciate his lean, muscular body, the wide shoulders that bore burdens well. She noted, too, the granite jaw that twitched with some emotion she couldn't identify.

After a while he spoke over his shoulder. "Is that hard, feeding him?"

"I'm a little sore. I think my milk's about to come in, though. According to Rosie, I'll need patience. Nursing is a learned skill. But he's a good little sucker." She stopped, smiled. "Rosie's words."

"Sounds like her. You seem like a natural."

She decided she had nothing to lose by being honest—and maybe something to gain. "It'd be easier if I didn't have to keep a blanket over me while you're here."

He stood instantly. "All you had to do was say so, Gina. I can go to another room."

"That's not my point. I'm staying covered up for your sake, not mine. I don't want to make you feel uncomfortable."

"You afraid the sight would turn me on?" He said it as if the idea was ludicrous.

Maybe I'm afraid it wouldn't. Stunned, she clamped her mouth shut. She had a hard time reconciling the fact she'd delivered a baby yesterday and was feeling some kind of powerful attraction to a man who'd rejected her once before. Rejected her soundly, coldly.

But that was then.

"I'm not worried," she said at last.

"If you don't mind, I don't."

"Thanks. I mean, it's not like we're strangers, right?" Now that she'd been granted the freedom, she didn't know what to do with it. She couldn't just whip off the blanket. That'd be like turning a spotlight on herself. Stalling, she took a sip of water from the glass she kept near all the time.

"Changed your mind?" J.T. asked, humor and challenge in his tone.

"Every first time is a little awkward, I guess," she said, watching him move purposefully toward her. Grateful only one lamp lit the room, she felt her cheeks burn when he peeled back the blanket. What the baby's head didn't cover, her nursing bra did, leaving only the slope of her breast visible. Joey suckled rhythmically, his mouth latched on tightly. She was aware of her other breast tingling, the one covered. Her nipple hardened as J.T. ran his hand along her son's head, cupping it, then raised his gaze to hers.

"What a beautiful picture you make."

The reverence in his voice turned her insides to mush. He leaned closer. Hope filled her heart. She tipped her head back, and then his lips touched hers, featherlight, a soft promise. He pulled back for a second, framed her face with his hands and returned for more, letting their breaths mingle, warm and enticing. A sound embarrassingly close to a whimper escaped her when he backed away again. She shut off his serious gaze by looking at his mouth, but her lips trembled open, anticipating, telling him what she wanted without saying the words, afraid she would beg.

A different kind of kiss, then. Longer and deeper, made all the more arousing because of his tender restraint. He seemed to be proving a point of some kind—to her or to himself? It had been so long since she'd felt needed, wanted. So long since she'd kissed a man. And this particular man had made her stomach flutter from their first eye contact. She'd chalked it up to strictly physical attraction back then. Could she now?

He broke off the kiss just as the baby's mouth went slack with sleep. Silence hung thick and heavy. Seeing his gaze drift down her, she squeezed her eyes shut, wondering what he would do next

"That should end any need for modesty," he said, low and gruff.

She nestled the baby a little closer. "I'll put him down. Then we can talk."

He offered his help to stand, then shoved his hands in his pockets at the exact moment she realized he was aroused, flatteringly so.

Every book she'd read assured her she wouldn't have the slightest interest in sex for weeks, at least, maybe even until long after the doctor gave his okay; that the baby demanded so much attention; that she would be tired. That the constant body contact between mother and child often satisfied the need for physical closeness.

The experts were wrong.

Warmth suffusing her, she met his steady gaze, pleased that he didn't apologize or offer excuses. But then, he'd always been honest with her, painfully so. It must have killed him not to tell her the truth when he'd found her huddled in front of his office.

"Hurry back," he said. "We've got a lot to talk about."

Right. He had questions, but she had some of her own. Like, why did you kiss me when you're supposedly "seeing" someone?

J.T. leaned his palms against the fireplace mantel and listened to Gina sing a lullaby as she put the baby to bed, the sweet, pure sound carrying over the baby monitor sitting on the coffee table. He hoped it worked for the baby, because it sure as hell wasn't helping *him* relax.

So much for the theory that giving birth voided sex appeal for a while.

She still had it. In spades.

Even worse, he hadn't been able to hide his reaction. So, now she knew she had power over him. What would she do with that knowledge? He'd hurt her twice before. Most people would want to even the score.

A flowery scent drifted into the room. She'd put on fresh perfume. For him.

"Deputy has decided to be Joey's nanny," she said from behind him. "They're becoming inseparable."

He turned around. She'd brushed her hair and changed her blouse. For him.

"He wouldn't get in the car with me this afternoon," J.T. told her. "That dog is going to be hard to live with when you leave."

Her shoulders drooped. Hell. Kiss her, then shove her out the door, why don't you, Ryker?

"You have questions?" she prompted, suddenly all business. Even the fragrance of her perfume dissipated, leaving only the acrid smell of his own idiocy.

With a gesture he invited her to sit on the sofa, but she chose her rocking chair instead, probably because of the cushion, but maybe for other reasons. He slid the ottoman next to her. "You were born to be a mother," he said, catching her off guard, forcing her to shift mental gears.

"It's what I've always wanted."

"Because you come from a big family?"

"Maybe in spite of it." She eyed him keenly. "We

don't have to ease into your questions, Chief. I'll tell you whatever you want to know."

Chief. Her way of putting him in his place. He reached into his pocket and drew out the condolence card he'd found in her trunk, then handed it to her. "You didn't just end up in Lost and Found. You were coming here. You said because you needed me. Why?"

"You took this from my personal belongings?"

"Max ordered me not to jog your memory. I was afraid the card would do that."

"Oh. Yes, he explained how I hid behind the amnesia because it reminded me of when Eric died."

"I didn't like keeping the truth from you, Gina."

"I know that much about you." She set the envelope on the table beside her. "I suppose to explain why I came to you, I have to go back to the beginning."

No. Not that far, he begged her silently. Not to the night we met. The first time I hurt you.

"To when Eric proposed," she said.

Not to the first time, after all. But to the second.

Six

Gina pictured Eric, a twenty-three-year-old, blond, attractive and charming L.A.P.D. rookie of four months. He'd worn the uniform proudly and well, with just enough swagger to make the leather of his gun belt creak when he moved. She'd loved the sound. She hadn't loved the fact he carried a gun all the time, even off duty, even on their two-day honeymoon in Las Vegas after their hasty wedding.

But he'd courted her zealously, dazzling her, somehow knowing she needed someone to pay attention to her.

She hadn't met anyone who'd wanted children as desperately as she—until Eric.

"Eric was an only child," she said to J.T., "as was his father. It was very important to him that the Banning name continue. So important that when he was eighteen he banked sperm, in case something happened to him that made him incapable of fathering a child.''

She appreciated that J.T.'s expression showed merely interest. But maybe he was accustomed to not reacting to people's eccentricities.

''He told me that the only wedding gift he wanted was a child to continue his name. I couldn't reconcile that with the fact he'd entered a line of work with a higher-than-average mortality rate.''

''That may be people's perception, but it isn't true,'' J.T. said.

''Yes, he assured me of that. It wouldn't have mattered, anyway. He believed it was his calling. Don't you feel the same way yourself?''

He seemed to retreat at the question. ''I became a cop for a reason, yes.''

''Then, you should be able to understand.'' She hesitated, considering his reaction, then a memory teasing her. Something Eric had told her about J.T. and a shooting, but the details were fuzzy. ''Anyway, his dreams and mine were the same, so it wasn't a sacrifice for me. I was more than willing to try to get pregnant right away. And more than willing to have his child if something happened to him. It was an easy promise to make.''

''So that dream you had about your father calling you a brood mare…?''

''The truth. Like the pot calling the kettle black, right? Look at my mom. Seven kids in twelve years.''

''And you were the fourth girl, not a novelty anymore, then followed by the first son. Did you get lost in the shuffle, Gina?''

His perception startled her. Her childhood was normal by most people's standards, and she'd been loved, if not for herself, for her mere existence. But she'd wanted more. "My parents did the best they could."

J.T.'s lips compressed but he said nothing.

She dug deep into her memories then. "After the accident I wasn't sure I would ever be able to carry to term. My injuries were critical. I'd lost the baby I was carrying. I never got to feel my baby move, but I knew it was there. And I loved it."

J.T. wrapped his hands around hers as she faltered.

"I needed around-the-clock care for a while, then extensive physical therapy for months. I moved in with my in-laws. Winnie, my mother-in-law, nursed me back to health. Then just about the time I was ready to be on my own again, my father-in-law died. I stayed on to help Winnie."

"And you never left."

"No. It was hard. She constantly reminded me of my promise. And I was haunted by the miscarriage. I kept dreaming of a baby crying, and I knew that the only way to end my grief was to get pregnant again. The first two times didn't take. Then, finally, the miracle happened."

"You got to keep your promise."

"And satisfy my empty soul, too. I was beyond happy."

"And your mother-in-law?"

"*Obsessed* wouldn't come close to describing her. She monitored my every movement, every phone call. I couldn't go anywhere without her. She hovered. She dictated. I kept trying to grow up, but she wouldn't let me. Every time I tried to break free of her, she became more desperate. My blood pressure skyrocketed. The doctor told me that if I didn't do something to change my situation immediately I could harm the baby and myself.''

''So you were right when you said you had to be protecting the baby,'' J.T. said.

''Always. My child will always come first. I'm sure my doctor didn't mean I should go so far from home, but I didn't see another option. I had to go where she wouldn't think to look.''

''To me.''

Such simple words. To me. Not, to Lost and Found. Not, to an old friend. To me. To him. Yes, him. In the time she'd known him, he'd confused her more than anyone she'd known, but she'd been sure he would help her.

''Yes. To you.'' She held his gaze for a moment. Their hands were still linked, and she rubbed her thumbs over the backs of his hands, feeling their strength. ''When Winnie made a quick trip to the grocery store, I wrote her a note, called my doctor to say I would be in touch after I settled in someplace, then I came here. I wanted to have time with my baby first, to learn on my own how to take care of him. Then I would contact Winnie.''

''So, what's your plan now?''

''I figure I've got three weeks before she becomes desperate. Until my due date.''

''You don't think she's looking for you now?''

''Of course I do. But I left on my own accord. The police wouldn't get involved, right? And I don't think she knows about you—that we were friends. Or that I would come to you.''

''You've said that before. Were we friends, Gina?''

She frowned. ''What would you call it? ''

''You said you hated me.''

Gina felt her cheeks heat up. "I came to realize that you were only looking out for me. Then I never saw you again to say I was sorry. I'd accused you of being jealous, when all you were doing was being concerned."

"Did I have reason to be?" His grip tightened on hers. His gaze bore into her. "Was he good to you, Gina? Were you happy?"

How could she answer that? Her expectations had been high. She'd thought Eric was her soul mate, but he'd changed after the wedding, becoming possessive, always making her aware that her primary duty was to have his child, to the point of nothing else mattering. He'd wanted her to quit college, to be accessible to him all the time.

"I'd known him a month when we got married," she said to the patiently waiting J.T. "Then we were married for only three months when he died. We hadn't had time for our relationship to settle in."

The baby started to fuss then, the sound coming over the monitor. Deputy padded into the room and stared at Gina. "I think he's trying to tell me something. And I'm kind of talked out, anyway."

J.T. helped her up. She stood on tiptoe and kissed his soap-scented cheek. "Thank you for listening. You were always good at that."

"Stop thanking me. It's no hardship."

She took a few steps, then turned around. "I think you're the only person who's ever looked at me, really looked at me when I talked." He was doing it again, she realized. Right that second. "Good night, J.T."

When the baby started to cry three hours later, J.T. was already awake. He'd barely slept since they'd gone to bed, instead listening for sounds from the next room, keeping at bay the old nightmare that had resurfaced upon Gina's return to his life.

No. She wasn't to blame. Guilt by association with Banning? That wasn't fair. But if it hadn't been for Eric, there would be no nightmare. No reason to quit the force.

That night in the pizza parlor might have turned out so differently.

J.T. stuffed an extra pillow behind his head as her voice, soft and soothing, filled the brief spaces when the baby stopped crying long enough to take a breath. He'd been pondering all she'd said earlier, trying to understand what drove her.

She'd taken too long to reply to his question about whether Eric had made her happy, then never really answered the question at all. "We hadn't had time for our relationship to settle in," she'd said. It seemed to him that the first three months of a marriage would be the happiest, the most exciting.

So, what did it mean?

His thoughts drifted back three years. Helpless, he'd watched Eric pursue her, had listened to him brag about how easily she'd fallen for him, like it was a contest and she was first prize. When Eric announced their engagement, J.T. agonized for days over what to do, finally convincing himself that since she didn't have any family around, someone needed to be a big brother to her. He knew Eric; she didn't. He wouldn't be too specific.

He'd gone to her dorm room, had tried to dissuade her from such a quick decision to marry, but she was head over heels, almost defiantly so, resenting his interference more than he imagined. He'd taken a chance, and lost. She would marry a man completely unworthy of her.

"He makes me happy," she announced. "And I hate you—*hate* you for trying to steal my happiness." She moved in on him, close enough that her perfume clung to his shirt afterward. "I think you're jealous."

He touched her for the first and last time, cupping her cheek, understanding that she was lashing out because he'd hurt her, hadn't treated her as an adult. Her eyes went black with emotions too complicated for him to sort, but not from anger alone. "I only want the best for you," he said honestly.

"He is," she insisted.

He made himself walk away, then hadn't seen her again. She and Eric eloped to Las Vegas the next week, and their social lives didn't mingle after that. But either she'd told Eric about their conversation, or he'd picked up on something, because his retribution came in a moment on the job that led directly to J.T.'s resignation from the force.

Hell. He punched his pillow, trying to get comfortable, not wanting to think about it anymore. The baby stopped crying midhowl. Gina yelped. Curious, he climbed out of bed and headed to her room.

He tapped on the door, waited to be invited in.

"Did we wake you?" she asked apologetically from among a pile of pillows. The top of the dresser had been converted into a changing table, a lamp beside it turned on low. "He has lungs, doesn't he?"

"I heard you shout."

"My milk came in. I'm really tender, and he latched on hard, then got a mouthful of milk. I'm not sure which one of us was more surprised, but his expression was so funny. Now he's just chugging away."

"Do you need anything?"

"Company." She patted the bed beside her. "I get a little worried that I'll fall asleep on him. I've never been so tired."

He stretched out beside her, leaned into her nest of pillows and watched the baby nurse. She wore an old flannel shirt of his, unbuttoned and flipped open on one side. Rosie had commandeered it because Gina's long nightgown didn't allow easy access to nurse.

The baby hiccuped, gulped and squeaked his way through the feeding. No one could stay detached watching him.

Gina laughed, said "Ow" a few times, and used her childbirth breathing techniques to try to relax. J.T. smiled sympathetically.

"You're a greedy boy, aren't you, sweetheart?" she crooned.

Not as greedy as I would be. J.T. put an arm around her. She stiffened for a second, then wriggled into a more comfortable position.

"I need him to change sides and relieve the pressure. I'm bursting at the seams."

Unable to utter a coherent word, J.T. rested his chin against her shoulder and watched as she maneuvered clothing and baby. She glanced in J.T.'s direction when her son was settled and suckling.

"Want to feel how hard my breasts are?"

He lifted his gaze, not saying anything.

"Go ahead. You won't believe it."

Shifting a little, he pressed his knuckles to her breast. "Whoa."

"I don't know why I'm laughing. It hurts like the dickens."

Fascinated, he spread his palm over her, sliding his

fingers under the fabric above her breast. She went silent and still. Joey continued to nurse, oblivious.

"How can something so...maternal be so damned sexy?" he asked, knowing it sounded perverse, but refusing to apologize for telling her the truth.

"That's the nicest thing anyone has ever said to me." She focused her gaze on her son again as J.T. moved his hand to cup the back of the baby's head. "Why haven't you married?"

"I don't have a clear-cut answer to that, Gina. I just haven't."

"Don't you want children of your own?"

"It's never been high on my list." Which was a simple answer to her complicated question, so he added a bit more. "I've seen a dark and ugly side of life."

"I know that being a police officer gives you a whole different perspective, but you have to have faith, J.T."

There was nothing he could say to that. Nothing. It wasn't only being a cop that made him see things differently. There was Mark, too, his brother, who'd lived so tragically, then died so violently.

"What about the woman you're seeing?" Gina said then.

Small-town gossip. Would he ever get used to it? "Rosie's information isn't up to date."

"Oh."

Just one word, but a lot of emotion packed into it, if he cared to break it down.

He didn't. "Will you be okay if I go back to bed now?"

"Sure. He's almost asleep, I think." She avoided his gaze. "Thanks. It's really nice being able to share everything with you."

"Yell if you need me."

"Okay."

At the door he turned around. "Did you tell Eric about our conversation?"

"Which one? The time you came to my dorm?"

He nodded.

"No. Why?"

"Just curious."

He gripped the door frame. Somehow Eric *had* known J.T. was a threat. After they were married, Eric gloated about her while he and J.T. were on patrol, about the fact he'd found the world's last virgin and how hot she was. J.T. changed the subject or tuned him out, but images burned, anyway—as Eric had surely intended.

"Eric didn't need to know," Gina said. "It was personal, between you and me. He would've read too much into it, plus you had to work together. As it turns out, I was wrong, anyway. You weren't jealous. Good thing I didn't say anything."

Trusting his instincts again, he walked back to her bed, no plan in mind, no words on his tongue, just a need to clear the air about that night.

She'd kept their conversation secret. He didn't know why that surprised him, but it did. And pleased him.

He started to thank her, but she looked at him with those deep, dark eyes that reminded him of the night they met. He leaned toward her, watching her, seeing need reflected in her steady gaze. No words, after all. He kissed her instead, without the restraint he'd used earlier, invading her mouth, feeling blistering heat in return, more than acceptance, beyond cooperation. Her sighs and moans fueled him. He dove his fingers through her hair, cupped her head, changed the angle of the kiss, searching, seeking, devouring, years of need released in one brilliant moment.

The pedestal he'd placed her on sank to ground level. Equals now, in passion and need. Just that damned age difference of a century or so, and a philosophical difference of more than that.

He still couldn't give her what she needed—children—and she wouldn't be happy with just one. But she also needed to know that he'd never judged her and found her wanting, as she'd believed.

He forced himself to stop, disciplined himself to walk away. At the door he looked at her, at the innocence still shining in her eyes after all she'd been through.

"I was jealous," he said, setting the record straight, not staying to see her reaction.

Rather cowardly, don't you think, for a knight of the realm? Mark's voice echoed in his head, as it had been too often lately.

In his bedroom, J.T. slid a photo of his brother from where it was buried in his dresser. Mischievous eyes. A charming smile. Brilliant mind. And all those demons inside.

"Just who the hell are you to speak of cowardice?" he asked his brother.

A silent taunt answered him, but it spoke volumes.

Seven

A chilling breeze blew Gina's hair from her face, the air stinging her cheeks as she walked into town for the first time, a bundled two-week-old Joey cuddled against her. His tummy full, he squinted against the sun. The distance from J.T.'s house to downtown equaled about two city blocks, not far enough to allow for much stalling, no matter how many times she stopped to point out a pine tree here or an interesting rock formation there. Deputy ran ahead then came back again and again, anxious to get there, but unwilling to let them out of sight.

Nerves gripped her. What would people think? That J.T. fathered a child out of wedlock? How had he explained her living with him all this time? Had he bothered to explain it at all? He was pretty closemouthed, an important quality in his job, if not in a mate. Of course, if what Rosie said about Lost and Found was true, no one would ask questions.

The town looked deserted. She could see J.T.'s car parked in front of his office, but that didn't mean he was there. He could be anywhere within walking distance. Maybe she should have called first.

A squawking blue jay dive-bombed Deputy, sending him into a barking frenzy. Startled, Joey exercised his healthy lungs with a few ear-piercing howls just as she stepped onto the wood-plank walkway that ran the length of downtown.

"Bad dog," she said to Deputy, who dropped his head and tucked his tail between his legs. Reduced to the status of a bully, she apologized. He seemed to grin, then hurried off, skidding to a stop at J.T.'s office to scratch at the door.

"This is not the best first impression, sweetheart," she crooned, tucking Joey closer, jostling him up and down, his cries sounding all the more loud as they echoed through the quiet town. Doors opened. People looked out. She felt her cheeks heat and hoped everyone would chalk it up to the nippy weather.

"Well, hello dear. You must be Chief Ryker's house guest."

A bird of a woman somewhere between eighty and a hundred signaled her to come into the shop, where Fabric, Craft and Ladies Undergarments, was painted in plain lettering on the window. Mrs. Foley, Gina decided, of the treed cat. Deputy would be smart to stay out of sight.

Gina introduced herself, soothed the still-crying Joey and was debating whether to accept the woman's invitation when J.T. stepped out of his office and headed toward her. She swallowed a sigh of appreciation at how wonderful he looked in his crisp uniform, his long legs bringing him quickly to her side.

Pleasure, or perhaps surprise, lit up his eyes. Ever since he'd admitted to being jealous over Eric, a piece of the wall between them had tumbled.

An even larger section remained, however. It was time they dealt with it.

"Hey," he said, taking the baby from her and cradling him with casual ease. "What's all the racket?"

Joey quieted. His head turned, seeking the source of the voice, finally zeroing in on J.T.

Aware of Mrs. Foley, Gina didn't tattle on Deputy, who took a few tentative steps closer, his tail wagging ever so slowly, then retreated when the older woman glared at him.

"We brought you lunch," Gina said to J.T. She slid a backpack down her arms, trying not to go all weak-kneed at the way he took care of her son, this man who'd never wanted children.

She had noticed, however, that he never called Joey anything other than "the baby" or "your son."

But for two weeks J.T. had silently appeared in the dark of night the minute the baby started to cry, scooping him up, talking as he changed his diaper, Joey going silent at the low-pitched, soothing voice. J.T. would hand him to her, stretch out beside them until the feeding was over, then return him to the bassinet. At some point he would kiss her, but always with the tiny human barrier preventing close contact.

His motives weren't entirely clear. At first she thought he was helping her stay awake, then she realized he liked being there with them.

"Did you meet Mrs. Foley?" he asked.

"Yes." She smiled at the woman talking nonsense

to Joey. "I'll come back another day, if you don't mind. It's our first venture out of the house, and I don't think either one of us will last too long."

"Come anytime. Bring the baby. He's the first one born in Lost and Found in thirty-eight years, you know."

Gina shook her head. No, no one had told her that. "Thank you for the invitation, Mrs. Foley. We'll be glad to visit." Unasked questions simmered in Gina's mind, but she respected the town's unwritten code by not voicing them. She walked beside J.T., offering a nod to the few people still lingering outside their shops. Unconditional welcome greeted her, quiet and steady.

J.T. shut the office door behind them. She glanced around the…room, she decided to call it, since it didn't look like any police station she'd seen. A couple of desks, several file cabinets, and all the normal electronic equipment necessary to run a business; bulletin boards tacked with wanted posters and other flyers. Three armchairs bolted to the floor comprised the makeshift jail he'd told her about once. On the rare occasion he took a suspect into custody, he would cuff him, buckle him into the front seat of his car, and drive him to the county jail, only a two-time occurrence in three years.

"This is a surprise," he said from behind her.

She didn't even have time to reply before Rosie swept into the office, lifted Joey out of J.T.'s arms without so much as a hello, then headed out the door, Deputy at her heels.

"We'll be back in a while."

"I'm fine, thank you for asking!" Gina called after her, earning a chuckle in return. She dropped the backpack onto a desk, aware of him watching her in the way he often did. Intense and focused. All consuming.

"Cabin fever?" he asked, coming up beside her and opening lids to the containers of food.

"Why won't you touch me?" She rounded on him, folded her arms under her breasts. She hadn't meant to be so direct—or strident—but she wouldn't back down, now that she'd blurted out her biggest question. She had others…

He mirrored her pose. "I touch you every day."

"No. You touch me at night, and only when I'm holding the baby. Never during the day. Never when our bodies might come in contact. Not even a hug hello or goodbye."

He frowned. "I wasn't aware of that."

"I'm *very* aware."

"Did it occur to *you* that you never touch *me,* Gina?"

Confusion zigzagged through her. "It would be too presumptuous of me."

"But not presumptuous of *me?*" He reached for her hand, flattened it against his chest, over his heart, holding it there. "I've read your childbirth book, remember? I know what to expect—and it's not physical contact."

"Well, of course I'm not ready to make love." She stuttered to a stop. "I mean, not that you're even interested or anything, but—"

"I'm not?" He lifted her hand to his mouth, kissed the pads of her fingers. "Who says I'm not?"

"You never touch me!"

"I'm touching you now."

She searched his face, trying to read his thoughts.

Here's a **HOT** offer for you!

Get set for a sizzling summer read...

with **2 FREE ROMANCE BOOKS** and a **FREE MYSTERY GIFT!**
NO CATCH! NO OBLIGATION TO BUY!

Simply complete and return this card and you'll get **2 FREE BOOKS** and **A FREE GIFT** – yours to keep!

Visit us online at
www.eHarlequin.com

- The first shipment is yours to keep, **absolutely free!**
- Enjoy the convenience of Silhouette Desire® books delivered right to your door, before they're available in stores!
- Take advantage of special low pricing for **Reader Service Members** only!
- After receiving your free books we hope you'll want to remain a subscriber. But the choice is always yours—to continue or cancel, any time at all! So why not take us up on this fabulous invitation, with no risk of any kind. You'll be glad you did!

326 SDL C26Q

225 SDL C26L
(S-D-OS-06/00)

▶ DETACH HERE AND MAIL CARD TODAY! ◀

Name: _____
(Please Print)
Address: _____ Apt.#: _____

City: _____

State/Prov.: _____ Zip/Postal Code: _____

The Silhouette Reader Service™ —Here's how it works:

Accepting your 2 free books and gift places you under no obligation to buy anything. You may keep the books and gift and return the shipping statement marked "cancel." If you do not cancel, about a month later we'll send you 6 additional novels and bill you just $3.34 each in the U.S., or $3.74 each in Canada, plus 25¢ delivery per book and applicable taxes if any.* That's the complete price and — compared to cover prices of $3.99 each in the U.S. and $4.50 each in Canada — it's quite a bargain! You may cancel at any time, but if you choose to continue, every month we'll send you 6 more books, which you may either purchase at the discount price or return to us and cancel your subscription.

*Terms and prices subject to change without notice. Sales tax applicable in N.Y. Canadian residents will be charged applicable provincial taxes and GST.

If offer card is missing write to: Silhouette Reader Service, 3010 Walden Ave., P.O. Box 1867, Buffalo, NY 14240-1867

BUSINESS REPLY MAIL
FIRST-CLASS MAIL   PERMIT NO. 717   BUFFALO, NY

POSTAGE WILL BE PAID BY ADDRESSEE

SILHOUETTE READER SERVICE
3010 WALDEN AVE
PO BOX 1867
BUFFALO NY 14240-9952

NO POSTAGE
NECESSARY
IF MAILED
IN THE
UNITED STATES

"I'm asking too much, aren't I? I can be really pushy when I want something."

Her words fanned a bright flame in his eyes. His arms slid around her. "I've wanted you since the moment you walked into the pizza parlor," he said, low and harsh. "I didn't see anyone but you."

His words confused her more than ever. "My life would have been so different if you hadn't rejected me. If you'd let me into your life. I wouldn't have given Eric more than a passing glance. No one had ever looked at me the way you did. No one."

His mouth brushed her temple. "Are you sorry you married him?" The words were almost whispered, and packed a big punch.

"I can't answer that." Would never let herself answer that. "I've hurt too much for too long. And I have Joey. I wouldn't trade that for anything. But I wanted to get to know you."

He leaned against the desk, settling her between his legs. "I had to stop it right then, when I learned how young you were. I had to. Gina—" he looked hard at her "—I would have eaten you alive. What I wanted from you wouldn't have fulfilled any dream you had."

She shook her head, again and again. "You're a kind man. Caring—"

"I was an angry man who got even angrier after that night. I would have hurt you beyond anything you could imagine. That's a fact."

"You've been good to me, and to the baby."

"I needed to make up for what I did to you."

Hurt spun a web around her heart. "I do not believe this is just your way of apologizing. You care. I've seen you with Joey. I've been in your arms. There's more going on than balancing some scales."

"Living in Lost and Found changes everyone."

"I've changed, too. But what hummed between us at the beginning hasn't faded with time."

"You want more children."

"Yes, I do. And you don't want any at all."

"Your son needs a father."

"I have needs, too."

He dragged his hands down her back, molded them over her rear, drew her against him, nestling her, proving a point. "This is why I don't touch you. You set me on fire. And I don't want you to think I'm pushing you—or that I can't control it. I can. *With distance.* You're not ready. I'm not even sure that I am. There's a lot we haven't talked about."

Which was true, Gina thought, even as she moved her hips a little, wanting closer contact. But it would be too easy to compare Eric and J.T., and not fair to either of them. Jumping into another relationship wasn't the answer. She couldn't give her heart again until she was sure that he wouldn't change after the fact.

She'd married for passion once, and the single common bond of wanting children. Friendship was more important, she'd discovered, and similar goals and expectations. Trust.

Her response to J.T. was too powerful to trust, always had been. And this was no time to be making decisions. She had yet to deal with her mother-in-law.

But first...

She laid her head against his shoulder, curved her arms up his back, pulling herself closer, so that she could feel him all the way down her body, enjoying the reaction he couldn't hide. He was so solid, so strong. She might stumble, but he wouldn't let her fall.

"Gina, you're killing me here."

"I need you."

He groaned, swooped low and kissed her, hard and deep and hot, lifting her into him, making love to her with his mouth—need at its most exhilarating; desire at its most dangerous; demand in its basest form. She reveled in it, not caring if the sounds vibrating in her throat seemed more animal than human.

J.T. dragged his mouth from hers. "You see why we need to keep things platonic?" he asked, pushing her back a little, cupping her shoulders as she swayed. "The book says you can't—that you won't even be interested for at least four more weeks."

"Guess I'm too greedy," she said, her hands fluttering, as if she had no idea where to put them.

He brushed her hair from her face. Her eyes shimmered. For him, this time. Only for him. Pleasure trickled through him like a hot spring through a snowdrift, melting the ice around his heart, flash-frozen long ago. "I always knew you'd be combustible."

"Then why did you brush me off?"

"I told you. We were worlds apart."

"But you never gave me a chance."

The truth of her accusation stung, as truth often did. Eric had walked into the pizza parlor moments after J.T. learned how young she was. If he hadn't been blindsided by his attraction to her—and the equally mind-numbing realization that he couldn't have her—he wouldn't have left her to Eric's practiced charm. Maybe she wouldn't have been so vulnerable, either. J.T. should have protected her from Eric. Instead, he'd been too busy guarding his own heart. His failure had cost her. She'd married fast, too fast. Had suffered. His fault. All his fault. And he'd always prided himself on being someone people could count on, even if he'd never known that comfort himself.

"I'm sorry," he said to her now, a blanket apology that she could apply to whatever he'd done that had hurt the most.

"You can make it up to me."

"How?"

"Just let things happen between us. We deserve to know what the possibilities are."

He linked hands with her, then rubbed his thumb over her wedding band, his gaze never leaving hers. As long as she wore the ring, Eric's shadow loomed. J.T. couldn't shake the feeling of being watched, and by a man whose actions would haunt him forever.

"I'm not ready to take it off," she whispered, acknowledging his silent question. "I'd look like an unwed mother."

"It's better to look like a cheating wife?" Regret sliced into him. He dragged a hand down his face. Swore. Apologized.

She turned away, busying herself with fixing a lunch plate. He noticed she didn't offer forgiveness.

"I'll bet you've said you're sorry to me more in these past two weeks than to everyone else altogether, in your entire life."

He thought that over. "You're probably right."

"Why? Are your expectations for me different from the average person?"

Taking her cue, he focused on the food. "With you I seem to speak first and think later. Although when I tracked you down at your dorm to talk to you about Eric, I'd thought it over for days, and I still screwed up."

"You didn't like Eric much, did you?"

He took a minute to think through his answer this time. "We had philosophical differences about the job."

"You didn't even come to our wedding reception."

"I figured the invitation was a formality."

"You were partners. It looked bad that you weren't there."

Partners. That was their departmental designation, but they'd never been partners.

Her spoonful of pasta salad shook a little as she piled it next to her turkey sandwich. Tension turned her spine rigid. Although she'd always seemed strong and independent, stubbornly so, her future now was unclear. She was a single mother, with an obsessed mother-in-law. Her family, who should have been her best support, had turned their backs on her.

He, perhaps more than anyone, understood how it felt to be that alone, not to have someone to lean on. Someone needed to take care of her until she was strong enough to take care of herself again.

And that someone was him. Whether he liked it or not, his duty was to protect her, a charge he'd given himself the night she'd landed in town. He wouldn't falter.

"Okay. I see that the subject of Eric is off-limits," she said without a glance in his direction. "But let me tell you this. Eventually I did appreciate the thought, if not the deed, of your concern for me. You didn't tell me I couldn't get married. Unlike my family, you tried to tell me why I shouldn't…yet."

He set his full plate on the other desk, then pulled up a chair for her. "I guess no one can talk someone out of getting married, but especially not a teenager."

"A teenager! How young that sounds to me now, an old lady of twenty-two."

"Think how it sounded to me then, when I was thirty-one."

"Oh, yeah. There should be laws against that kind of age difference."

He eyed her. "I was an old thirty-one. And you were a young eighteen."

"I've matured." She looked around. "Where's your rest room?"

He pointed the way, then watched her walk down the short hallway. She'd complained a couple of days ago that she still couldn't quite button her prepregnancy jeans yet, but he could see she'd lost most of the baby weight. And he'd overheard Rosie grumble yesterday about the elasticity of young skin and Gina apologizing for it—in words, if not in tone. In fact, she'd sounded pretty close to bragging.

"Brat," Rosie had called her.

"Jealous," Gina countered.

"Just you wait. After your second, you'll see how much harder it is to lose the tummy. And after you're done nursing this one, you'll wish for the days of perky breasts and bras without underwires."

"My badges of honor," he'd heard Gina say.

He didn't know about later, but she looked plenty perky to him now. Plenty.

The door opened. Expecting Rosie and Joey, he was surprised when a woman walked in, a stranger. He registered her statistics: late forties to early fifties, average height and weight, short blond hair, styled, but not fussy. Gray wool pants and a matching sweater. A black overcoat.

An attractive woman, if her expression hadn't announced her intention to do battle. He'd seen it often enough in his career.

"Come in," he said, standing. "I'm Chief Ryker. What can I do for you?"

Her gaze slid from his.

"Hello, Winnie," Gina said from behind him, her voice strong and steady. "Welcome to Lost and Found."

Eight

Panic lit the woman's eyes as she focused on Gina's flat stomach, then scanned the office. Horror seeped in. "The baby. Where's my baby? Oh my God. Something happened—"

"No. Winnie—" Gina stepped toward her "—he's fine. He's just fine."

Everything happened so fast then. Winnie took a step toward Gina, desperation in her eyes, an animal sound in her throat. J.T. locked an arm around her, immobilizing her.

"No! Don't! Let her go, J.T. Please. Let her go," Gina implored. "Let go." Softer then, but even more insistent.

"I'll cuff you to the damn chair, if I have to," he said to Winnie, close to her ear.

He released her, but didn't move away.

Gina extended her hands toward her mother-in-law. "You have a grandson, Winnie. And he's beautiful."

"Where are you hiding him?"

Gina flinched at the icy accusation. After all these years, didn't this woman know her daughter-in-law at all? *Hide her baby?*

"He's with a friend," Gina said, as if the strain of staying calm hurt. "A nurse. They'll be back soon, I promise."

"He's ill?"

"He's perfectly healthy."

"Get him."

Gina shifted her gaze to J.T. He shook his head. He wasn't going anywhere.

"Why don't you have a seat. I'm sure they won't be long," Gina said.

Winnie glared at J.T., then perched on a chair. "When was Eric born?"

"January second, just past noon. And his name is Joey. Joel Eric Banning."

She almost levitated from the chair. "We agreed! If it was a boy, he was supposed to be named Eric."

"No, Winnie. You announced it, deed done. I never agreed. He needs his own identity."

"I won't call him that. Joey." Her mouth pinched tight.

"Yes, you will."

J.T. heard something new in Gina's voice—authority. She looked a little different, too. Composed. Serene.

"You'll call him by his given name, because I'm his mother, and that's my choice. He's his own person, not a replacement. I promise you he'll know everything there is to know about Eric."

"Well, a promise from you isn't worth much, is it?"

Gina crouched in front of her. J.T. went on full alert, ready to intervene, earning himself a long, level, dagger of a look from the woman.

"I kept the ultimate promise," Gina said. "It wasn't easy on me. I've miscarried. I've had the equivalent of two more, when the inseminations didn't take. I went through a pregnancy alone."

"You had me."

"I mean, without my husband, whom I loved and needed."

Her declaration wrapped around J.T.'s throat and tightened. He'd never heard her say the words before. The past would never fade for them, he realized. They would always be tied by it, by what they had in common—Eric. By her love for him—and J.T.'s hatred. By the child that was a living link, who couldn't be ignored.

Gina set a hand on Winnie's. "I know you did the best you could. But your best was too much."

"I have rights."

J.T. snapped to attention. "Legally you have no rights," he said, glad the law backed him up. He could see why Gina had left. His blood pressure would've skyrocketed, too.

"I do have rights. And I know who you are, J.T. Ryker. My son never trusted you, and I see he was right. He knew something was going on between you and his wife. He knew."

"Then he was full of crap."

Winnie gasped.

"And so are you," he went on, "if you think I'm going to let you get away with insulting or intimidating her. I'll slap you with a restraining order."

"A toothless threat," Winnie said, haughty. "My husband was a cop. I know that Gina would have to initiate a complaint. She won't."

The fight for territorial control over her struck Gina as ludicrous. She laughed, the sound building hysterically as she bent over, holding her stomach, escaping their matching expressions of alarm. They thought she'd lost her mind. Maybe she had. Maybe three years of grief, sacrifice and emotional roller-coaster rides had converged into one massive attack of insanity.

She got herself under control as sounds of an unhappy baby filtered into the building, gathering volume when the door opened and Rosie breezed in.

"Not a happy camper," she shouted. "He's had enough oohing and ahhing, I think. Max said you must be feeding him pure cream. He's gained fifteen ounces."

Winnie rose unsteadily. Gina's throat burned at the need she saw, and the instant, unconditional love.

"Rosie, this is my mother-in-law, Winnie Banning. She'd like to hold her grandson."

The precious moment imprinted itself in Gina's memory. Winnie lifted him into her arms. He cried louder. She paid no attention, her eyes welling up, spilling over. She pressed her face to his, kissed his forehead and cheeks, then held him so she could look at him.

Deputy growled, his ears back. Winnie tucked the baby close.

"It's okay," Gina said. "This is Deputy. He's just not used to Joey crying this long. I need to feed him."

"Where's his bottle? I'll do it."

"I'm nursing him."

"We agreed—"

Gina shook her head. "But you can hold him when he's done." She looked at J.T. in silent question.

"Rosie, what do you say we get a cup of coffee?" He picked up Deputy and carried him out after one final behave-yourself-or-else look at Winnie—and a wishful glance at his uneaten lunch.

Then they were alone, Joey's cries filling the room, along with enough tension to shovel. Gina hoped her milk would let down with Winnie there. Grateful that nursing was easy for her now, she settled him with a minimum of fuss, then smiled at the ferociously hungry sounds he made.

"He's a good eater," she said to Winnie. "He'll nurse hard and fast, then fall asleep exhausted."

"Like Eric."

"Really?"

The older woman nodded. Tentatively she cupped the back of Joey's head, but he was used to it with J.T., so he didn't even break rhythm. "Eric played hard. Slept hard. Ate like Trojan." She flashed a quick look at Gina. "I never in my life struck Eric. Or anyone."

Gina accepted the implied apology. For Joey's sake she would make this relationship work. "I understand that you were scared. But I hope you'll see I didn't have any other choice." She told Winnie about her blood pressure and the doctor's concerns. "I'm sorry I had to resort to running away. I would've called you soon, honestly. I just wanted time with Joey first. Can you understand that?"

"Frankly, no. I can't believe you see me as such a witch."

"Well, we don't have to talk about it now. You're here. Joey's healthy. Everything turned out fine. How did you find me, anyway?"

"You have to promise not to get mad."

"I do?" She smiled at Winnie. The woman did mean a lot to her. She'd forgotten how much, actually. Winnie had given up a year of her life to care for her while she recovered from her injuries, never once complaining about the total disruption to her life. "Okay, I promise."

"Dr. Gold called to pass along your message that you'd had the baby and were fine and would be in touch. I waited. I waited some more. Then I couldn't stand it anymore. So I bribed the file clerk in his office to look in your file and see if there was a contact number. There wasn't. But he'd noted that you were living in Lost and Found, and who your doctor was here. I was going to call whatever police authority was in charge, then I learned that the chief was J.T. Ryker. The same J.T. Ryker who was my son's partner."

Gina decided not to tell her about the accident and the amnesia. "He was the only person I could think of who would help."

"Why not your family?"

"You would've contacted them. I didn't want them to lie for me."

"Well, your parents are worried sick. I hope you've called them."

"Actually, I haven't." *I've been living in a dream world, but I guess that time is over.* Back to reality. She didn't know if she was ready to face it, but she guessed she didn't have a choice. She wanted a fresh start. She wanted everyone to see her as a mature woman. A good way to begin was by assuming her responsibilities. "I'll call them today."

Winnie plucked at the baby's blanket, her nerves showing. "This J.T. seems pretty protective."

"Eric was wrong, Winnie. There was nothing be-tween me and J.T. I loved my husband."

A long pause ensued, then Winnie said, "He was a hard person to live with."

Finally someone said the words out loud. "Yes," Gina whispered. "Yes, he was."

"So was his father."

Their gazes met and locked, then Winnie reached out and hugged Gina, the baby fussing a little between them.

"I'm sorry I suffocated you," Winnie said.

"I'm sorry I didn't speak up." Gina smiled at her. "We'll start again. We need you, Winnie."

"Good. Now, how soon can you be packed and ready to go home?"

"You told her she could *what?*"

Gina didn't cringe from J.T.'s bellow, even though she'd never heard him raise his voice before, and it shocked the daylights out of her. Rocking just a bit faster, she soothed Joey, who'd been so startled he'd let go of her nipple and was rooting for it. She helped him find it again, then said to the towering, impatiently waiting man, "I told Winnie she was welcome to spend the day here tomorow." Looking up at him, she smiled as his gaze dipped to her breast and he lost his train of thought altogether.

After a minute he crossed his arms and frowned. "You had no right. This is my house."

"You'll be at work."

She decided she kind of liked him angry. He wasn't angry at her, after all, but at the situation. And the fire it put in his eyes appealed to her.

"I don't trust her."

"She's not a bad person, J.T. She just didn't handle things well."

He strode to the fireplace, tension coiled in him, so that his walk was different. Rigid.

"She tried to force you into leaving. You're not ready to leave."

"No, I'm not, and I told her so. But I can't deny her time with Joey."

"Damn Mrs. Foley for offering a room at her house." He stabbed at a log with a poker. "It's her way of paying me back for Deputy chasing her precious cat."

Gina smiled. Really, she did love this side of him. Passionate. Illogical. Human. "If Mrs. Foley hadn't offered, Winnie would've found another solution, even if it meant sleeping in the car."

"I can't come home for lunch."

"Of course you can. You'll just have to accept that she'll be here, too."

"For how long?"

"Why don't we just wait and see how it turns out."

"Why don't we just set some ground rules to start with and make her agree to them."

"J.T., even I don't know how long I'll be here."

He went still. After a minute he spoke over his shoulder. "You can stay as long as you want."

Forever? The word hovered, settled, warmed. "Thanks," she said instead, leaving it at that. He was so different from Eric. Gina tried to picture Eric doing any of what J.T. had done since she'd dropped into his life. Cook? No way. Clean? Woman's work. Change a diaper? That was good for a laugh. "I'm a guy!" Tolerate postpartum tears, the highs and lows? "It's all in

your head,'' he probably would have said, patience not
his strong suit.

He would've loved his son, though.

Winnie's words about Eric—and his father—being
hard to live with had comforted Gina. She would have
felt disloyal saying them to his mother, yet the admis-
sion had cemented a tighter bond between them. Now
if she could just get J.T. and Winnie to like each other,
everything would be perfect.

Why does that matter? a voice inside her asked.

She closed her eyes as the answer hit her with the
intensity of a thousand-watt bulb. *Because I've fallen
in love with him. I've fallen in love.*

The revelation hurt more than it satisfied. It wouldn't
be easy, loving him. Not easy at all. She would have
to fight his history with Eric—and her—his unwilling-
ness to father children, and whatever memories haunted
him, destroying his ability not only to love, but to be
loved.

And she still had a niggling worry about him changing after, like Eric. She'd already witnessed a new side
of him tonight, although one she liked.

One thing was certain: if she told him she loved him,
he would accuse her again of being impulsive. Maybe
he'd been right before, but not this time. She'd come
to the conclusion on her own, not because he'd
charmed her into it, or pressured her, like—

She sighed. *Don't compare, Gina. Look at J.T. for
what he is: steady and reliable, passionate but not
overwhelming. A true partner.*

Every dream come true. Provided he was willing to
take on Eric's child.

''Joey's asleep,'' she said, standing, needing to get
away, to think. ''And I'm exhausted, too. I know it's

only nine o'clock, but I'm going to take a shower, then go to bed."

"Here, give him to me. I'll burp him and put him down. You go on."

Gina transferred the sleeping baby to his arms, then looked up at him, seeing him differently now. His eyes seemed more golden, as if a brighter flame lit them. And his face was more dear to her, his mouth more tempting. What would it be like to belong to him, body and soul? Would he ever let her find out?

"I was proud of how you handled Winnie today, Gina. You were something to see."

His good-night kiss was a disappointing brush across her forehead. After the scorcher they'd shared in his office today, she'd expected their relationship to change somehow. Maybe it had. Maybe Winnie's arrival had changed everything.

Well, he wasn't going to get away with it. Locking her hands behind his head, she pulled him down and kissed him until he took charge, turning the kiss into an all-out assault, his free arm yanking her closer.

The man sure could make love with his mouth. Desire burst out of dormancy. She wanted him naked against her, where she could touch and see and feel. She needed to run her fingers through the hair on his chest, glide her palms down his hard, flat stomach, wrap her hands—

He dragged his lips from hers, groaned her name, panted as they touched foreheads. She tried not to whimper. He couldn't overwhelm her? How completely wrong could she be?

"You'd better go," he said, shaky.

She mumbled some garbled reply, tried again, then gave up when he didn't smile, but looked at her like he was addicted to chocolate and she was the last truffle in the box.

Her knees wobbled as she made her way to the bathroom and stepped into the shower, then she stood under a cool spray until she shivered. Four weeks to wait until he used more than his mouth. Four more lousy weeks.

"Mrs. Banning."

"Chief Ryker."

J.T. opened the front door a little wider, inviting her in with the motion, words of welcome stuck in his throat. He'd hardly slept, reliving the fiery kiss at first, then anticipating the changes Winnie Banning would bring. He'd paced, held a fruitless, one-sided conversation with his brother's sarcastic ghost. Then he'd wandered outdoors and leaned against a porch railing in the thirty-five-degree night, wearing only sweatpants and a T-shirt. Nothing helped. He wanted her.

And he wanted her mother-in-law to go away.

"Gina's in the kitchen," he said to the irritant now. "Have you eaten?"

"Hours ago," she snapped, implying how long she'd been made to wait.

After Gina went to bed the night before, he'd called Winnie and told her not to show up before nine o'clock. She'd sputtered, but finally agreed. J.T. acknowledged his own selfishness. He'd come to enjoy the mornings with Gina. She would be gone soon enough. He was damn well entitled to savor her now.

"I figured you'd be at work by the time I was *allowed* to see my grandson," Winnie said.

He'd planned to be, but her belligerent tone ticked him off. How Gina could stomach the woman was beyond him. "I'll go when I'm ready."

Her mouth drew into that pickled expression she'd carried around with her yesterday. J.T. led the way to the kitchen.

"I thought you were leaving," Gina said as he walked in. Then she smiled. "Just Teasing?"

The private joke jarred him, as had her mood all morning. She'd smiled at him more. Sent him undecipherable messages with her eyes. And that kiss last night...

He'd pretended to sleep through the middle-of-the-night feeding, just to avoid her. She hadn't called him on it yet, which bewildered him even more.

"Oh! Good morning, Winnie. I didn't see you behind J.T." Gina hugged the woman. "Joey should wake up famished soon. Would you like some coffee?"

Too much domesticity, J.T. thought. What the hell had happened to his quiet life? "I'll eat lunch at Belle's," he said, for an instant wishing he could kiss her goodbye in front of Winnie. The spiteful thought irked him even more. He'd regressed to adolescence because of her.

He jammed his hands in his pockets. "See you later. Come on, boy," he said to Deputy.

The dog moseyed over to stand next to Gina, his tail wagging slowly. "Sorry, man," his eyes seemed to say. "I'm not goin' anywhere."

Hell. It was bad enough the women had taken over his house, but to witness Deputy's snub, too? His own dog, a traitor, and a disgrace to his gender.

J.T. gladly escaped. He made his customary drive to check out the town, the routine calming. People waved. He didn't stop to talk to anyone, as he usually did. By now word would've spread that Gina's mother-in-law had descended. Who knew how much she'd told Mrs. Foley.

Enough to arouse interest, he discovered when he parked and headed to his office. People milled through downtown, a sly glance here, a grinning "Morning, Chief," there. Not his imagination. They treated him differently.

He swore as he swept into his office, swore as he started the computer, swore as he grabbed pages from the fax machine.

Max chose that moment to visit.

"How the hell am I supposed to maintain authority if everyone loses respect for me?" J.T. almost shouted. "I have never been a source of gossip for this town. Never."

Max dropped into a chair. "Good morning, J.T. Having a bad day?"

"Don't mock me." J.T. slammed a file onto his desk. "Don't you have patients to see?"

"Not at the moment."

Max's placid response forced J.T. to get himself under control. He flipped through the fax pages. "People need to know they can count on me."

"Everyone knows that. But that doesn't mean they're not curious. This is ten times more interesting than television."

He gave up any pretense of working. "My life has become a soap opera, Max."

"I'm looking forward to the next installment, myself."

With a snort, J.T. sat. He rubbed his face, then let his arms drop to the desktop.

"You're looking a little peaked, J.T."

"Lack of sleep." Lack of privacy. Lack of routine.

Lack of sex.

He heard himself growl. Max had the nerve to chuckle.

"I'm an idiot," J.T. said, chagrined. "Can I ask you a question in confidence?"

His friend eyed him thoughtfully. "No, you don't necessarily have to wait six weeks after childbirth to have sex. Some women heal faster than others."

Grateful for Max's perception, J.T. took it one step further than he would have. "How will we know?"

"I'll advise her to come in at the four-week mark. We'll see. I take it she's as anxious as you."

"We haven't discussed it."

"I never figured you for an avoider. J.T., I can give her the okay physically. Beyond that, it's up to the two of you. Just remember that she can get pregnant, even though she's nursing." He glanced at his watch and stood. "And, Chief? Just because I don't tell anyone about our talk doesn't mean they won't know what's on your mind. Everyone will be happy for you."

"I'm not sure it's going to make me happy."

"Then maybe you'd better wait until you know."

Nine

Good. Winnie's car was gone. J.T. loosened his death grip on the steering wheel as he pulled into his driveway. For a week they'd uttered civil hellos and good-byes. For a week she'd offered unasked-for advice about baby care. He and Gina had done just fine on their own, as far as he could tell. Still she harped about the baby not being dressed warmly enough—or too warmly. They'd had a huge argument over how he was supposed to sleep—on his back or stomach. Winnie hadn't believed that putting babies to bed on their backs lowered the number of deaths from SIDS, not until J.T. produced proof.

"Well, in my day we put them on their tummies," she'd said in a huff.

"I'm sure in your day you gave birth in the fields then went right back to tilling," he'd muttered, prompting Gina to choke on a laugh and Winnie to eye him sourly.

The past few days she'd stayed for dinner, too, so he'd had to put up with her for an hour that he could've spent in more agreeable company, with Gina. She'd seemed happy, truly happy, this past week. He had to give credit to Winnie for letting her nap each day. And maybe having another woman there was a comfort that he couldn't provide. He only knew that she smiled a lot more.

He took a minute to greet his turncoat dog in the kitchen before going in search of Gina. He found her in the rocking chair, feeding the baby, who made noises so loud J.T. could hear them from across the room.

"Hi," she said softly, her face lighting up.

She looked so perfect, so serene. Joey's fist thumped her breast, his fingers opening and closing. One bare foot stuck out of the blanket and flexed up and down. He must have just started eating, because he was obviously wide awake.

J.T.'s heart did a slow somersault. Feelings he'd been fighting surfaced fast, a painful lack of oxygen squeezing him from inside. Maybe he could take a chance. Maybe in this town he watched over he could have a future with her. With them. He couldn't give her more children, but she might be willing to settle for the one.

Eric's child… No. Gina's child.

His jaw clenched. And Eric's mother—part of the package.

Plus, all those things he could never tell them about Eric. But keeping secrets was something he was good at.

"What's wrong?" Gina asked. "Why are you frowning?"

He shut down his thoughts. Tonight was for them. He walked across the room, cupped her face, tipped her head back and kissed her thoroughly before pulling away an inch or so. "Hi, back," he said.

"Well."

Offering the baby his finger to hold, he propped his fist against her breast and kissed his downy head, then his tiny, bouncing foot.

"I guess you're glad to see us," Gina said.

"More than I can say." Without pulling his finger free, he slid the ottoman closer and sat. "Did Winnie go home?"

"Don't look so hopeful. No. She was invited to attend the Women's Club meeting tonight."

"She doesn't strike me as a 'club' type of woman."

"Actually, she was active in several organizations before she quit to care for me."

"No job?"

"Her husband left her well-off. Although I think it would be nice if she'd either get a job or get busy with her groups again. She's only forty-nine. The social outlet would be good for her."

The babe fidgeted, lost the nipple, then howled until he found it again.

"Such an impatient little piggy," Gina said, smiling.

"How about you, Gina? Did your husband leave you well-off?"

She didn't look at him. "His insurance did."

"So you won't have to work?"

"Not unless I want to."

"What about college? As I recall you had a full

scholarship to USC. You wanted to be an elementary school teacher.''

''My scholarship was for soccer. Can't do that anymore.''

''Do you want to go back to college?''

''Someday. For now my job is right here in my arms. It's a luxury a lot of women would envy.''

''You probably envy a lot of women what they have, too.'' A husband, a home.

She looked out the window.

''How was your day?'' she asked after a while, switching the baby to the other side and pulling her bra flap over her breast.

Their hands bumped as he hooked it, trying to be matter-of-fact, but not succeeding, not inwardly, anyway. ''My day was interesting.''

''I-in what way?''

He'd shaken her up a little. Good. ''I got a call from the county sheriff. I told you we have a mutual aid agreement, right? And with the other police and fire districts nearby, too.''

''I remember.''

''Well, there was a bank robbery in Alta Tierra, which is a dinky little town about thirty miles south of here. The sheriff didn't really think the suspect would head higher into the mountains, but every department was put on alert. Sure enough, about noon he comes into town. Pulls up to Barney Cochran's gas pump. Now, Barney's a go-getter, you see. Some traveler comes through, he's going to make sure that oil and water gets checked. Air in the tires. The works.''

J.T. stretched out the story, and his legs. ''I called it in, then took my time making my way over there, not wanting to draw attention to myself. My first priority was to keep Barney from getting caught in a cross fire, but I also knew that Barney wouldn't let this guy loose anytime soon. I figured he'd be sent off to Belle's for lunch and told to come back in half an hour. The guy would find his car gassed, watered, aired and washed, no charge except for the gas, which is already hiked up for our convenience of getting gas here. That's Barney."

Gina was smiling. He sat a little looser, enjoying having an everyday conversation with her.

"Needless to say, the suspect was in a bit of a hurry. They get into an argument when Barney reaches into the car and pops the hood latch to check the oil. The guy goes ballistic. He rams the hood back down, grabs some bills out of his pockets—a couple of hundreds, by the way—and tosses them at Barney. By the time he's climbed into his car, Barney's got the hose turned on to give the car a quick wash, whether he likes it or not." He laughed. "The driver's window was open. Guy got drenched. When I got him out of his car, he was a human icicle. Funniest thing I'd seen in ages."

Her eyes sparkled. "You really love this job, don't you?"

He fingered the hem of her blouse, lifted it to his nose. Flowers. Gina. "I make a difference in Lost and Found."

"You didn't make a difference in L.A.?"

"Not like I do here."

"You said once before that you became a cop for a reason."

It was his turn to stare out the window. Would talking about it end the nightmares for good this time?

From beside her and under the baby's blanket, she

pulled out a picture frame, holding it toward him. "Who's this?"

She'd taken the decision out of his hands. A part of him was relieved. "Where'd you get that?"

"I did laundry today. I was putting yours away in your dresser when I saw it. If this is you as a teenager, I think I'm glad I didn't know you then. He looks like the kind of guy women would do anything for."

J.T. lifted it, cradling the frame in his hands. "He was."

"Was?"

"My brother, Mark. He died fifteen years ago."

She laid a hand along his face, but he didn't take his gaze from the picture.

"I'm so sorry. I didn't even know you had a brother."

"He still talks to me."

She barely hesitated. "What does he say?"

J.T. set the picture on the end table beside her, taking his time, choosing his words. "He thinks I'm too noble."

"What do you think?"

"He's probably right. But I am what I am."

"You were close?"

"You can't get much closer. Identical twins. Mirror twins, to be specific."

Gina glanced at the photo again. Yes, she could see it now, not just a resemblance but a duplication. Erase fifteen years and it would be J.T.—except for the mischievous expression. "How did he die?"

He rubbed his face. When he pulled his hands away, he looked a decade older. "The official term is suicide by cop. It was on our twentieth birthday."

Her stomach clenched. Why did some people choose

important days to kill themselves and other people hang on somehow until a holiday had passed?

"I hardly know what to say, J.T. I can't begin to imagine it." The baby had stopped nursing and was deep into sleep. She shifted him to rub his back, but she wished she could hold the man sitting in front of her, to soothe him as easily as Joey.

"Mark had always been different. Difficult. From early on he had no control over his impulses. After years of medical evaluations he was finally diagnosed with bipolar disorder. Manic-depressive, most people call it. As a child he would eat until he was sick, because he never knew when he was full. He hardly slept. The older he got, the less he slept. He'd wander the house at night, all night. Would wake me up to talk, and he'd go on and on and on. He was incredibly talented artistically, and would paint for seventy-two hours straight sometimes, creating horrifying, vivid scenes, each one more macabre than the next. Then he'd come down from the manic state and sleep for a long time."

"The watercolors in your bedroom—did he paint those?"

He nodded. "You wouldn't know it was the same person. During his letdown after a wild episode he would do these beautiful seascapes, in watercolors instead of oils." He patted Joey's back, as if needing the connection. "Women flocked to him from the time he was twelve. He was charming and flirtatious and very mature for his age. If he wanted something, he could figure out a way to get it, and if charm didn't work, insistence did. You have to understand he had no self-control. That was his tragedy."

J.T. pushed himself up and prowled the room. Gina ached for him.

"The experts know more about it now, that it's a chemical imbalance. And in his case he'd started experimenting with drugs, which only worsened his condition. He was finally accurately diagnosed when he was eighteen, relatively young. Usually the worst of the symptoms are just starting to appear about then. And when he took the only medication that ever worked for him, lithium, he seemed almost normal. But he hated taking it. Said it blunted his creativity. I know this sounds crazy, but I could hear his thoughts sometimes. I knew when he was putting on a show. Sometimes I could talk him down mentally, but often he was beyond even my reach."

He leaned his hands against the mantel, his body stiff. "He unraveled. That's about the only way I can describe it. He bought a gun. Then he taunted a cop, threatening him until the cop had to shoot to save himself."

His voice went deathly quiet. "I knew the moment the bullet struck him. I knew the second he died. The noise in my head stopped so suddenly I thought I'd gone deaf."

God. Oh, God. She laid the baby on the sofa and went to the man, insinuating herself between him and the hearth, holding him as hard as she could, crying for his poor, sad brother. Crying for the devastated man left behind to keep living, one half of a whole. The sane twin. The duty-driven twin. The one who always put everyone else's needs ahead of his.

Finally he wrapped his arms around her, taking comfort. "I don't have any tears left for him."

"Is that why you became a cop?"

"I figured I could identify the ones with mental illness. I knew the signs better than most." He tucked her closer. "I didn't want it to happen to anyone else. Not if I could stop it."

The phone rang, the sound so jarring they jumped apart. He turned away before she got to judge whether talking to her had helped at all.

His conversation was brief, ending with, "I'll be right there."

"Old John," he said over his shoulder, his strides long and hurried. "He's drunk and getting mean. I'll be back."

It would probably take an act of Congress to get him to talk about it again, Gina thought, watching his car speed off. And she wanted to ask him about a time when another man was shot by a cop—by him. Eric had told her about it. She'd almost forgotten, because it had happened just a couple of weeks before the accident. J.T. had put in his resignation soon after.

Not a coincidence, Gina decided. Not at all. He'd become a cop for a reason. He'd failed, at least in his mind. The man he'd shot had at least left a note behind.

But knowing J.T., she could see how it would make him quit. And knowing him, too, she could see why he'd moved on to another police job, but one where he could get to know everyone personally, to identify problems and solve them before they became too tangled.

To give his brother's death meaning.

Okay. She would listen if he wanted to talk, but she wouldn't bring it up again. He deserved to bury what he could.

At least she knew what he was fighting.

Ten

Winnie Banning had no intention of leaving town without Gina and the baby. J.T. came to that conclusion after her visit dragged on a second week and she immersed herself further in the town's business and social life. Her current obsession was to spearhead an effort to start a library. Next on her agenda was Meals on Wheels, a program she'd led in her community before Gina's accident.

He thought the woman needed to get a life, but he'd counted on it being in Los Angeles.

His office door swung open with a whoosh of cold air. "Will you sign me off now, Chief?"

J.T. set down his copy of *PORAC,* the police publication he'd been attempting to focus on. Fourteen-year-old Jeremy Burton stood with his hands jammed into his pockets, his hair hiding his eyes. Today marked the completion of thirty hours of community service, his sentence for vandalizing several downtown stores with graffiti. On top of cleaning up the graffiti, he'd been ordered to serve five hours at each business he'd damaged. J.T. had gotten the biggest kick out of watching him work off his time at Kathy's Kut and Kurl, figuring Jeremy's horizons were broadened most by his five hours there.

"I don't expect to see you in my office again for anything other than reporting a crime or applying for the cadet program," J.T. said, standing.

The boy's closed expression twisted into confusion. "I can be a cadet?"

"When you're sixteen. If you keep your nose clean."

Jeremy swiped a hand across his mouth. "Promise?"

The question said a lot about the boy. J.T. clamped a hand on his shoulder. "Promise. You'll have to cut your hair some."

The teenager shook his shaggy locks out of his eyes. "No sweat."

"You did a good job, Jeremy. Everyone said so."

"My mom woulda killed me if I hadn't."

The door opened behind Jeremy, winter surging into the room again. Winnie stood there, the baby snuggled in a pack against her chest. Great. His day was complete.

"See ya, Chief," Jeremy said, a hesitant smile on his face.

"Stop by and say hi now and then, okay?"

"Sure. Bye."

"I thought you and Gina were headed to Sacramento to do some shopping." J.T. crouched a little to look at the baby, who was sucking on his fist, his eyes open.

Joey smiled, something he'd started doing regularly a few days ago. Yesterday he'd laughed for the first time.

"It's three o'clock. We've been there and back," Winnie said, then thrust a piece of paper at him. "Here."

He unfolded it, wary of what he would find.

"Everyone on that list is donating books for the library. I figured you could pick up the boxes while you're on your rounds."

"You give up your driver's license?"

Her stare was stony. "I thought you could store them in your garage, since you never park your car in it."

"Oh, you thought—"

"I noticed a bunch of books in your home office you might think about donating, too." She cocked her head. "Funny. I figured you for a murder-mystery and home-repair kind of reader, not poetry and certainly not Shakespeare."

The books were Mark's, who'd had eclectic interests. Parting with the volumes meant giving up a tangible piece of his brother, who'd devoured everything in print, memorizing passages with ease and quoting them so cleverly that the object of his scorn never heard the insult behind it. J.T. had admired and been appalled by Mark's brilliance.

"So much for a man's home being his castle. Where's Gina?"

"She had a doctor's appointment. Should be done—"

J.T. didn't hear the rest. It'd been four weeks. He'd been counting the days, but she hadn't mentioned the appointment. His imagination soared with possibilities. Tonight, Gina? Finally?

"Chief Ryker. Are you not paying attention or just being rude?"

Winnie wielded her tongue like a saber. Hell, no, he hadn't been paying attention. Would Gina tell him she'd gotten the okay? Would he have to guess? They hadn't talked about it, but the unspoken expectation came through in every kiss. It was only a matter of time...

He returned to his desk and tried to look busy. "Was there something else you wanted, Mrs. Banning?"

"You can start by calling me Winnie, for one thing, so that I don't feel like an old lady."

"It's a sign of respect."

She made a sound of disbelief. He stopped a laugh just in time. Really, the woman was too easy to ruffle.

Gina breezed in. He examined her for changes, saw nothing. No blush to her cheeks, no hint of *tonight's the night* in her eyes. Neither did she look disappointed. Helluva time not to be able to read her expression.

"I need a nap. Shopping wore me out," she declared, then knelt to pet Deputy, who'd thrown himself at her.

J.T. saw it as a sign of Deputy's good taste that he hadn't taken to Winnie. One look from the woman could reduce him to a quivering mass of canine obedience, but not friendliness.

"Would you like to eat out tonight?" he asked Gina. Start the evening with a little romance. A little candlelight. Some quiet conversation. Winnie would be glad to baby-sit, he was sure.

"I've already thawed the chicken. But thanks for the offer."

Strike one. Well, maybe she wasn't the romantic type. Or maybe she didn't want Winnie to acknowledge they might have more of a relationship than…housemates, or whatever it was they were.

As they departed, Winnie sent him an eyebrows-raised, lips-pursed look of…what? Curiosity? Triumph?

Damned if he didn't feel like every kind of fool.

After dinner, after Joey was fed and put down, J.T. loaded some soft, slow music in the CD player and invited Gina to dance. It was the ultimate sacrifice, in his mind, all for the sake of romance. He hadn't danced since high school.

Her hesitation spoke volumes, even if he didn't hear any specific words. After a minute she accepted his hand and moved into his arms, but held herself stiffly. At the end of the song, she pleaded exhaustion and hurried out of the room. At eight o'clock.

Max must not have given her the okay.

Strike two.

Well. He'd been wanting to catch up on his sleep. This looked to be a perfect night for it.

Panicked, Gina bent her head close to the bassinet and listened. She strained harder, not hearing anything. She laid a shaking hand on his tiny chest. There! Okay. There. Breath. In and out. Steady.

Safe.

She gripped the nearby dresser until her legs could support her again. Her heart stopped thundering. Relief pushed at her eyes, wet and hot.

The bedroom door creaked open. "Did I sleep through him crying?" J.T. asked.

She straightened instantly, not wanting him to see her weakness, her fear that something would happen to the baby, too—second only to her fear that something would happen to *her*. Who would raise him? It had begun to haunt her.

Hushing J.T., she set her hands at his waist and backed him into the bathroom, pulling the door shut behind her. "He hasn't woken up yet."

"But it's three-thirty, an hour past his usual time."

"He's a month old, you know. I guess he's starting to sleep a little longer. We're supposed to be glad."

"Oh. Now what?"

"We go back to bed. He won't be shy about letting us know when he's hungry. And Deputy's a good backup alarm."

"Will you be able to sleep?" he asked, a frown forming as he looked hard at her, seeing too deep for comfort.

"Sure."

He didn't say anything for a few seconds, then he grabbed her hand and tugged her along. "Come with me."

No lights were on in his bedroom, but the curtains were open and moonlight streamed through the window, pale and low.

"Get in bed," he said. "I'll light the fire."

It was the first she'd known him to use the fireplace in his bedroom. Obedient because she chose to be, she slid under his blankets as he turned on the gas flame under the logs.

He glanced over his shoulder. "So, how scared were you?"

She blew out a breath. "I broke records getting to his bassinet. My heart was pounding so loud I couldn't hear him breathe for a minute."

''I didn't figure you were as calm as you looked. I wasn't.''

She snuggled deeper into his pillows, inhaling the scent lingering there. ''You didn't look calm, J.T.''

''Yeah. A whole different adrenaline surge from what I'm used to. I think I prefer the one that comes from facing an armed robber.'' He padded across the room, lifted the bedding and climbed in beside her.

She tried not to react, but a drum roll sounded inside her.

He moved back until he rested against the headboard. ''Scoot over here between my legs. I'll give you a back rub while we wait for Joey to wake up.''

He had great hands. Anticipating, she moved into place, then it struck her that he'd called the baby by name for the first time. What did that mean? Did it mean anything?

''Take off your shirt.''

What? She swallowed. ''What?''

''The room's warm. Gina,'' he said close to her ear, ''from the waist up, nothing about you can surprise me anymore.''

He might as well have asked her to do a striptease for him. Nursing the baby was a natural, normal thing. Well, maybe she was a teeny bit more aware of J.T.'s eyes on her than at any other time, but she'd learned to set aside modesty, because it was the practical thing to do. This...

This was different.

Mentally picking up the scattered pieces of her courage, she unbuttoned the shirt, letting it slide down her to her hips. Even in the heated room, goose bumps rose on her flesh. She jumped when he touched her.

''You can trust me.''

"I know."

Then his fingers slid under her bra, there was a little pull on the fabric and she was unhooked. Free. Exposed. Even if all he could see was her back.

It felt good, so good, although totally impractical.

"I've got to leave my bra on. I'm leaking because I'm anticipating feeding Joey," she said, regretting the return to reality, grateful she wore underwear. No romance here, she thought with a sigh, wishing otherwise.

She heard rustling behind her, then his T-shirt, still warm from his body, fell over her shoulder and into her lap. "Set that under you. Gina, everything is washable, including us."

She closed her eyes, enjoying the skill of his strong hands and fingers. He never hurried, not even in this. Methodical, meticulous and thoughtful—that's how she would describe him, tossing in *independent* and *appealingly stubborn* for interest. He wasn't given to wild displays of temper or mood swings, nor did he make unreasonable demands of her.

"I don't know how I'm ever going to repay you." She'd jammed some pillows in front of her to lean against, and they muffled her words. "I've taken and taken from you, without giving anything in return."

"I'm not keeping a tally."

J.T. trailed his fingers down her back, knowing he would have to stop at some point, but deciding she should know his intentions, in case she had any doubt. There was no reason to rush, however, and every reason to savor.

Time ticked by. Although they didn't talk, he knew she hadn't fallen asleep but had completely relaxed. Appreciative little sounds told of her pleasure and her gratitude. After a long while he let his fingertips graze her sides, barely touching where her flesh turned softer and decidedly curvy—and greatly aware of the Reserved for Baby sign that might as well be tattooed on her.

She made a new kind of noise in her throat when he ventured slightly farther, then she raised up a bit in a subtle invitation. Sliding his hands around her, he caressed her ribs, drawing her against him. She sucked in a breath and arched her back when he finally cupped her breasts, enjoying the solid weight resting in his hands. He brushed his thumbs over her nipples in a feather-light touch.

"I'm sorry," she whispered, hunching. "I'm so— This is not in the least romantic."

She really didn't get it, he realized, didn't know that everything about her excited him. "Turn around."

He waited as she sorted the situation in her mind. One step at a time, he cautioned himself. Be patient. Let her come on her own terms. They could only go so far tonight, anyway.

Dragging his T-shirt with her, she faced him, her gaze leveled at his chin.

He slid his legs together, forcing her to straddle him, her fingers digging into his shoulders as she fought for balance. Grasping her hips he steadied her for just a moment, her silky underwear heating like fire.

He waited, watched. Wanted. Didn't touch, except with his eyes.

She lunged at him, wrapped her arms around his neck, her mouth pushing against his, her tongue seeking entry. Lowering her hips, she settled on him, nestling, groaning. The sound slipped from her to him, the vibration skimming down his body, centering where they touched.

"No," she moaned, burying her face into his shoulder.

"It's all right. Shh. It's all right." He enveloped her, held her close. "I know we can't do more until Max says okay."

Her mouth moved against his shoulder. "He said okay."

J.T. went still. "What?"

"Today. I went to see him. He said we could, if we wanted."

"But—" He held her shoulders and pushed her back. "You didn't even give me a hint."

"I was afraid I couldn't stop!"

He counted to five. "Now tell me something that makes sense."

"I went shopping today because I wanted to buy something beautiful to wear for when the time was right. I didn't have any idea Max would release me this soon. I didn't buy anything, because Winnie never left me alone for a second. I didn't want her to see! It's private, between us."

"Hell, Gina. You think what you wear makes a difference to me?"

"It makes a difference to me."

Women.

Strike three. By legal standards, he'd just been sentenced to prison without a possibility of parole.

Somehow he hung on to his patience. "I was trying to put a little romance into the evening, too, you know. Dinner out. Dancing in. I wanted to make it special."

"That's so sweet." She pressed her hands to his face, her thumbs to his lips. "But look at me, J.T. Look at yourself. I've dripped—'' She stopped, clamped her mouth for a second. ''It could get even messier if I...you know.''

Joey started to cry, although with more fuss than fury. J.T. placed a hand on Gina's arm as she started to get out of bed, relief in her eyes.

''Don't make the mistake of believing it's got to be perfect, okay? That's a lot of pressure on both of us.''

After a moment she nodded. The baby's I-want-to-eat-*now* cry kicked in.

''You can feed him in here. I'll get him,'' he said, knowing she would cover up while he was gone, sorry that they'd lost what had been building between them.

Amazingly, she'd only drawn his flannel shirt over her shoulders, and the picture she made as she nursed the baby burned into his memory. When Joey fell asleep again, she scooted off the bed and left, without saying a word.

He stretched out on his back, his arms pillowing his head, knowing he should get up and turn off the fireplace. Instead, he listened to the sound of water running in the bathroom, then silence. Out of the corner of his eye he caught a movement—Gina, walking toward him. He pushed up onto his elbows, enjoying the view of her still wearing his shirt like a cape, the exposed inner curves of her bare breasts moving slightly with each step. Her stomach was only a little round. Her eyes asked and answered questions, their dark depths glittering.

She didn't look like anyone's mother.

Her fragrance fused with the warmth of the room, lingering, enticing. Silent, she knelt beside him, then dragged a warm, wet washcloth over his chest. He lowered himself to the bed again and closed his eyes, enjoying the luxury, not moving until after she'd patted him dry with a towel. Her hair brushed his stomach as she pressed a kiss to his chest, right over his heart, then she flattened her hand there, trapping the kiss.

"When it comes down to it," she said, "your shirt is the most special nightgown I've ever owned. I always feel like I'm sleeping in your arms all night."

"Then you won't mind if I replace it with the real thing?"

She shook her head.

He slid the garment down her, wadded it up and tossed it out of reach. She'd slipped out of her underwear before she came back to him, and faced him now, temptingly natural, tantalizingly bold.

And his.

He stood long enough to shove his sweatpants down and off, then knelt before her. Such a long time he'd wanted her. Such a very long time. His hands shook as he touched her hair, following the silky length to the curls at the end, then lifting the thick strands over her shoulders, out of the way. She shivered.

"Cold?"

She shook her head, her eyes on him.

"Anxious?"

A flicker of a smile.

"You might as well relax. This is gonna take a while," he said, reminding himself to go slowly, to be careful with her, gentle, even as a storm of need whirled inside him, gathering power and strength.

It doesn't have to be perfect.

The reality lingered in his mind, but fantasy demanded its fair share. Perfection was his goal.

He wove his fingers with hers, lifted one hand to kiss the tips of her fingers, the inside of her elbow, the hollow of her throat as she arched and sighed. He dragged his open mouth down her breastbone, imprisoning her hands by her sides, waiting for her to stop him with a word. She arched a little higher, angled to one side. Freeing her hands, he cupped the bounty she offered, made a trail with his tongue over and under. Across.

Should I? he asked by pausing.

She went completely still. "Don't stop," she whispered.

"Just for a minute. Just to know what you feel like," he said, gruff, needy.

"Yes. Yes."

She felt like a miracle. Creator of life. Heavy with sustenance. Woman, pure and giving. Hard and soft. Sweet and hot. Better than his dreams. Real, finally. Something he could touch and taste, not the need-spun fantasies that had begun years ago, an obsession finally being satisfied.

Attuned to her, he knew when to move on, and did, rising a little above her, capturing her mouth, pulling her body against his, the kiss a wild torrent she returned with fervor. Her hands glided down his back, curved into his rear. She tipped her pelvis higher, seeking, begging.

"Not so fast," he murmured.

"Why not?"

The plaintive sound made him smile, slow down, savor. She flattened her palms on his face, kissed him hard, dragged her hands down him. He felt something catch in his chest hair.

Something…

Her wedding ring.

Her damned wedding ring.

His eyes on hers, he captured her left hand and held it in her sight line. "He can't be between us, Gina."

"I know."

"If it comes off, it stays off."

She didn't hesitate a second. "It comes off."

He closed his fingers around the wide gold band. She shook her head.

"It can't be you," she said. "It has to be me."

Eleven

With the ring gone it couldn't be their secret. Winnie would know. Everyone would know. And yet Gina wasn't sure herself where this turn in the relationship would lead, only that she needed to take it.

Someone had to take a chance. It wouldn't be him. He was too logical, too accustomed to putting everyone else first. To take, just because he wanted? Not part of his code. She had to be the one.

Aware of his searing gaze, she tugged the ring off her finger, opened the drawer to his nightstand and dropped it in, a solid plunk of metal to wood, the death knell of that relationship, her mourning long ago given up privately, but now publicly.

Before she could shut the drawer, he wrapped a hand around hers, rubbed at the indentation the ring left, then traced his tongue around it like a brand. Wonder rocketed through her, trailing fire. The world shimmered and shined.

He wouldn't offer words of love yet. That truth was inescapable. Nor could she give him the words that waited in the wings of her heart, not until he was ready to hear them. He might take duty too far.

"Gina."

He waited for her, calm, patient. Or was he uncertain? Did he really think she would change her mind? That she would come this far, only to stop? The man was a saint if he could. She couldn't, even though she was a little fearful about how her body would accept him.

"Make love to me," she said, arms extended in invitation. "With me."

He matched his body to hers, legs twining, hips aligned, the soft hair on his chest brushing her breasts.

She said she was ready. With a soft press of lips to her temple, he murmured, "Not yet."

He started with her mouth, ended with her toes. Along the way, exploration, discovery, temptation. He was tender and demanding, yielding and resistant. He loitered over every caress, assaulted her senses, handcuffed her modesty.

She insisted she was ready. He hovered above her, stroking, testing. "Not yet," he said. Her groan of frustration made him smile, not gently but with knowledge of the power he had.

She'd thought him fierce before? Nothing, *nothing* compared to now. His intensity was the brightest she'd seen, a crystal bulb about to shatter into a billion shards.

He asked everything of her, wouldn't settle for less—not only from her, but himself. She finally stopped thinking and lost herself in him, in the textures of his body, so different from hers. In the beauty of his masculinity, a life force, giving and taking. "Ready," he breathed, then, strong and hot, he eased into her. Instant explosion. Another. Too much. Oh, too much. His mouth on hers, liquid fire, drowning sounds, then soliciting new ones, louder, longer, lower. No, those came from him.

She'd done that? She had the same power as he?

Ah, yes. She felt exhilarated in her power. Found joy in his satisfaction.

Then their two suns collided, creating a new universe, minuscule but theirs. Only theirs.

Heaven on earth.

J.T. rolled over, needing to keep her wrapped in his arms, but knowing he was too heavy to stay on top, a flesh-and-bone blanket. His mind barely functioned. Nothing had ever compared.

"I never knew it could be this good," she said against his neck.

Ahh. Thank you, Gina. Every curiosity satisfied in one simple, generous statement. No need to wonder.

Her generosity demanded reciprocation. "Do you know what day this is?" he asked, kissing her fragrant hair, stroking her back, reveling in the little shudders he generated.

"The first day of the rest of my life?"

Her warm, lazy tone didn't completely hide the deeper question, one he had no answer to. He had to think through the consequences, had to know if she would be willing not to have more children. He hadn't been so swept away that he'd forgotten to use protection.

"My birthday," he said.

She lifted her head, propped her arms on his chest. Still dazed at his good fortune, he trailed his forefingers over her cheekbones, down her face, along her jaw.

"This is the first time in fifteen years I haven't spent it celebrating—commiserating—with whiskey."

"You? I've never seen you drink anything other than a beer."

"Once a year." *And one other night. The night you told me you hated me.*

"Grief changes us. I've learned that much."

Finally, someone who didn't utter platitudes or offer advice. Grief was the least of it, after all these years. Anger, frustration and helplessness all jockeyed for first place. If he could get his brother to stop talking to him... "Maybe this year I'll just get drunk on a bottle of Gina," he said. "Aged to perfection."

"To the legal drinking age, anyway. By my calculation you've got about nineteen hours of birthday left, and you've only drunk down to—" she touched her shoulder "—here. That's not even enough to make you tipsy."

"I'm feeling no pain. How about you?"

Gina pressed her nose to his chest and inhaled him. "I think you went out of your way to make sure of that."

"It was important. It still is. Gina, look at me, please."

She did.

"I'm counting on your honesty. If anything makes you uncomfortable, you have to tell me. It matters."

"I'll try."

He sat up against the headboard, taking her with him, repositioning her to straddle his lap. "You have to do more than try. And you need to tell me what you like, too.''

She didn't know how to voice such thoughts. She had no reason to be shy with him anymore, but she also had no experience with someone who cared more about her satisfaction than his own. ''I liked everything you did,'' she told him honestly, and then she kissed him, as much in gratitude as in need. ''I was a little nervous that it might hurt, but after a while I forgot I was worried.''

''The ultimate compliment.'' He drew her close to kiss her again. ''I don't suppose we could tell Winnie we're under quarantine,'' he muttered against her mouth.

She laid the back of her hand to her forehead and closed her eyes. ''I do feel a tad feverish.''

''I have a cure for that.''

''Does it involve a cold shower?'' she asked. ''Because I've had enough of those lately.''

''No wonder we never ran out of hot water.''

''You, too?''

He smiled and nodded.

''Maybe it wasn't so bad that we had to wait a month,'' she said, brushing his hair with her fingers.

''Plus three years. I slept with you that first night a hundred different ways in my mind.'' He angled his head, kissed her throat.

''Are...are there a hundred ways?''

He moved lower, dragged his tongue between her breasts, filled his hands with her, plunged his teeth softly into the plump underside of one breast. She arched, letting him support her, feeling deliciously wanton. Low in her body he pressed hard and hot against her. She rocked a little. He drew a long, slow breath.

"Self-control," he said, as if remembering then and reminding himself now.

"Tell me one of those hundred things you wanted to do," she said, feeling daring.

"If I do, will you tell me something, too?"

"From that night?"

"From that night. From before we actually talked."

"And you flat rejected me."

He sighed. "You were a teenager, Gina."

She wrinkled her nose.

They were in need of a little mood shift, J.T. decided, wanting to return to the intimacy of a minute ago. He slid his hands over her rear, pulled her closer.

"Once, you leaned over the pool table, your eyes on me instead of setting up your shot. Do you remember?" he asked.

"Which time?"

"The time you crooked your finger in invitation—"

"I've never crooked my finger at anyone!"

"Whose fantasy is this?" As the memory flooded him, he moved her against him, the friction driving him wild, the freedom intensifying every sensation. "I lifted you onto the edge of the table, then I ripped your T-shirt clean down the middle—" he mimed the movement, made a sound of cloth tearing "—tossed your bra into the hanging lamp overhead, peeled your jeans off and took you, spread out on the pool table. Hell, Gina. A leather jacket. Boots. All that tough-girl surface, and good-girl underneath. Every man's dream."

He lifted her, impaled her.

She gasped. Went still. Closed her eyes. "You fill

me up so much it's hard to breathe," she said, her voice shaking.

"More compliments. No, don't move. Just sit there and let me look at you." He waited until she opened her eyes. "You don't know how many times I pictured you like this. Whenever you were in the same room. Sometimes even when you weren't."

"You mean—" she held her breath as he slipped a hand between them, exploring and arousing "—all those times we saw each other after that, the polite conversations we shared in the middle of rowdy parties—" she groaned as his thumb circled her ever so slowly "—you were thinking things like that about me?"

"Those were my tamest thoughts."

"Um—" she tipped her head back, made a long, low sound "—um, I never knew."

"I didn't want you to know." He held her motionless then, afraid he would lose control, and he hadn't put on protection.

"Being near you excited me," she whispered, tightening around him, fighting his resistance. "I felt so disloyal."

"Attraction is chemical. You can't control your body's response, only what you do about it. And, Gina, you have nothing to be ashamed of." He let her move awhile. Stopped her again. Loved the sound of her protesting groan. "Now tell me something."

Her eyes glazed over, then cleared slowly. "You'll laugh."

"I won't."

For a few long seconds she said nothing, did nothing. Finally she wrapped her arms around him. "You seemed like the loneliest man I'd ever seen. I just wanted to hold you and comfort you and tell you everything would be all right."

No, he didn't feel like laughing. Lonely, yes. Alone. If he'd known she would satisfy more than physical needs—

No. She'd been eighteen. Eighteen.

He pulled back a little. He couldn't remember having a conversation while he was inside a woman. Pleasure rocked him. "That's not a fair trade of stories, Gina."

She smiled, then bent low. Kissed him right over his heart. "My thoughts weren't as explicit as yours. I didn't have much experience to draw on. You scared me back then, if you want the truth."

He held his breath as she trailed her tongue over his chest, lingering here and there, tempting, arousing. Deep inside, she convulsed around him.

No protection. The reminder flashed through him like lightning. Keep talking. Stay distracted.

What *were* they talking about? "Ah. Ticked off. You were ticked off at me."

"Only when I had good reason to be." She sat up, encircled his neck with her arms. "Until then, when you made love to me with your eyes, I was afraid I was going to let you."

"I knew how attracted you were."

"You did?"

He dragged his hands down her breasts, ran his thumbs over the peaks. "These got hard every time our eyes connected for more than a few seconds."

Her face paled.

"Which is probably why I didn't stop to consider how young you were."

She swallowed. "Well, at least I did something

about it. I invited you to shoot a match with me. You would've sat there all night, staring.''

''I wouldn't have let you walk out without finding out who you were.''

She kissed him, a hard, rhythmic caress...high and low, then eased back, her eyes filled with passion and tenderness and a whole lot more that he didn't dare put a name to.

''This is the most personal conversation we've ever had,'' she said. ''If I'd known it only took getting you naked to get you to talk...''

He didn't give her the satisfaction of a response, but flattened her on the bed, made quick work of protecting them, then drove into her. ''Okay?'' he asked when she sucked in a quick breath.

She raised her hips, nipped his shoulder. ''Better than that.''

Unleashed of restraint, he gloried in her eagerness, wallowed in her earthy scent, exulted in the untamed coupling. He demanded; she acquiesced. He captured; she capitulated. He took; she gave. Hot need bubbled from a cauldron of carnal innocence that annihilated the past. No other man for her, no other woman for him. Rebirth. A primitive union but pristine and pure.

Their voices merged, souls mingled, hearts united. She was his. He was hers. No truth was greater than that.

The family bed. J.T. smiled at the scene of Gina feeding Joey, the baby cuddled against her bare skin, doing a chorus-line kick with one spindly leg. Deputy, stretched out beside them, resting his head on her thigh.

''Isn't this cozy?'' she asked, her eyes sparkling in the way he remembered.

"It's quite a picture." He set two mugs of coffee on the nightstand, shifted Deputy closer to her feet, then sat beside her. Draping an arm around her, he captured Joey's foot, and the baby smiled at him around the nipple, milk dribbling down his face before he latched on again.

"What are you thinking?" she asked.

"How beautiful you are."

"You always know the right thing to say." Relaxed and unselfconscious, she nestled her head in the hollow of his shoulder. What a difference a few hours made.

No, he didn't always know the right thing to say. That was one of his problems. He was working on it, though.

When the baby was done nursing, she climbed out of bed and headed toward the bathroom. The view of her naked behind teased and tantalized. He would've followed her except that Winnie was due soon, so he lay there instead, focusing on anything other than hauling Gina back onto the mattress.

After a minute she peeked around the doorjamb and crooked her finger at him. With as much self-will as a hypnotist's subject, he followed.

"Uh-uh. Recommended attire is your birthday suit."

He shoved his sweatpants off, kicked them out of his direct path.

"Aren't you even going to ask what's up?" she asked.

"I think that's obvious."

She laughed, sweeping her gaze down him in appreciation.

"Where's Joey?" he asked.

She held out a hand. He drew her into his arms instead and kissed her, slow and sweet.

"Um, Joey's in his bassinet. He'll be happy long enough for us to take a shower. Together."

"Winnie's due to swoop in on her broomstick pretty soon."

She gave him a playful shove. "I called her and told her not to come until nine-thirty."

He walked with her to the shower, his hand lingering at the small of her back. "What excuse did you give?"

"I said you'd had a hard night and had gotten a late start."

He turned a faucet, waited for the water to run hot. "A hard night?"

From behind, she hugged him, her breasts soft against his back, her hands gliding down his chest, his abdomen...and beyond.

"A very hard night," she said, her voice husky. "Which seems to have continued into day."

"Lucky me."

He had planned to be gone by the time Winnie showed up, but he'd gotten two phone calls, delaying him by ten minutes—nine minutes too long. They'd already been cutting it close when he'd carried Gina from the shower, tossed her soaking wet onto his bed and took her with a speed and force she not only encouraged but matched. They had lingered afterward, speaking quietly, touching tenderly, until they couldn't dawdle a second longer.

As he walked now from his office to the kitchen, where he could hear the women talking, it occurred to him that he should be grateful to Winnie. If she hadn't made life hell for her daughter-in-law, Gina wouldn't have gone in search of him.

Prepared to be generous to the woman, even

friendly, he stepped through the kitchen door and said good morning.

She sat at the kitchen counter, Joey cradled in her arms. Gina was in the utility room, but carrying on a conversation about how the baby had slept six hours between feedings for the first time. She came into the room, balancing an armload of folded laundry.

Her hair was still wet. His was damp. There hadn't been time to blow dry. Winnie glanced from him to Gina, her brows drawing into a deep vee. Then her eyes zeroed in on Gina's hand. Her ringless hand.

Winnie's face turned white. Gina wasn't watching, was probably avoiding making eye contact. J.T. schooled his features.

"Can I pour you a cup of coffee, Winnie?"

Her eyes opened wider at his polite offer. "No, I—" She stood, handed the baby to J.T., then took a few backward steps toward the door. "I only stopped by—"

Her voice shook. She had the look of a cornered animal.

"I've got other plans for today," she finished. Then she left without a goodbye and hurried to her car.

Gina set the laundry on the counter, her eyes bleak. She rubbed her bare finger. "I shouldn't have let her go like that. I should've made her stay and talk."

"The worst is over now. Give her time to accept it."

She nodded. J.T. kissed Joey's head, passed him to Gina, then kissed her hard, reminding her why she took the ring off. He could have stayed a while longer now that Winnie was gone. He didn't punch a time clock, after all. But he'd gone from a single to a couple a little too fast for comfort, and he needed time alone. Maybe Gina did, too.

Tonight he would <u>tell</u> her why he couldn't give her more children.

Tonight he would find the right thing to say.

Tonight.

Twelve

She fixed pot roast with browned potatoes and carrots, a ton of gravy and an apple pie with birthday candles stuck into those little vent slits on the top crust—not thirty-five of them, but enough. It was the best meal J.T. had eaten in, well, maybe forever.

The last bite consumed, he pushed himself back from the table and groaned. "How'd you know?"

She stabbed a piece of pie crust on her plate, turning it into crumbs. "Know what?"

"My favorite meal."

She tapped her temple. "Woman's intuition."

He contemplated the way she annihilated the crust, indicating nerves of some kind. "You called Belle."

A flash of surprise crossed her face, then she smiled. "Great deduction, Chief. She challenged me to a bake-off, by the way. Her apple pie against mine. Blind taste test by the city council. I didn't know there was one."

"We don't hold city elections. People volunteer. They keep the position until they get tired of it, then someone else steps in. Aaron Taylor's been the mayor for seventeen years, I think." He stood when she did, scooping up dirty dishes to carry to the kitchen. "The biggest controversy I've heard about was when some city slicker—their words—tried to build a hunting lodge and resort over the ridge. Lots of people here hunt, but it's to feed themselves, not for sport."

"It's a very nice town, J.T."

"It grows on you." He set the dishes in the sink. *Has it grown on you, Gina? Enough to stay?*

"You won't win the bake-off with Belle." He smiled at her offended look. "The citizens of Lost and Found are loyal to their own."

"How would they know which one is hers?"

Placing an arm on either side of her, he trapped her against the sink as she rinsed the dishes and nuzzled her neck. "'Cause yours is so much better."

"Good answer, Chief."

Reaching past her, he flipped on the radio, found a slow country tune. "I believe you owe me a dance. One where our bodies actually touch."

Staying within his human barrier, she turned to face him. "That was merely self-preservation, as you'll recall. A sacrifice of the highest order."

A kiss first, he decided. Then another as they danced...longer, an invitation to more.

He leaned close. The phone rang.

Muttering one pithy word, he snatched the receiver off the hook and snarled a hello.

A brief silence greeted him, then, "Happy birthday, Son."

It took him a couple of seconds to change gears. "Mom. Hi."

Gina loaded the dishwasher as he talked to his mom, then his dad. His voice was strained at first, then he settled down, leaning against the counter and making more than just polite conversation. She'd talked to her parents today, too, for the third time since Winnie's arrival. Her father had apologized for calling her a brood mare. Her mother wanted to visit, but Gina put her off, not knowing whether J.T. would think she was being presumptuous inviting her to his house.

"Where'd you go?" He wrapped his arms around her as she stared out the kitchen window, wringing a dishcloth over and over. She leaned against him, tossed the cloth in the sink.

"Just thinking about family, how complicated those relationships can be," she said, enjoying the moment. How lovely to share life with him. How very lovely.

"That's the first time I've talked to them on my birthday since Mark died. They always call, but I never pick up. It was selfish of me. They were grieving, too. I heard it in their voices on the answering machine."

"You invited them to visit?"

"All these years, they waited to be asked. Helluva son I am."

"They understand. I know they do."

"They feel guilty. Mostly because they couldn't figure out what was wrong with Mark for so long, although it wasn't for lack of trying. But also because they thought I got lost in the shuffle. Mark got all the attention, because he demanded it."

She linked fingers with him at her waist. "Were you lost in the shuffle?"

"Yeah. Sometimes." J.T. shifted a little, uncomfortable with the memories. Mark had an illness. How could anyone get mad at someone for that? "He liked to call me the good twin. He was the evil one, of course. But sometimes I would get furious with him and I'd yell that I was the evil twin, like it was a compliment or something." He closed his eyes. "Then I'd get scared that I was becoming like him."

"Which is why self-control is so important to you."

It was the perfect lead-in for the discussion he'd planned...

"And it's why you quit the force after you shot that man," she added.

After a paralyzing flashback of the moment he'd had to fire, J.T. moved away from her, busying himself by washing his hands. The symbolism didn't escape him—he had blood on his hands he could never scrub away.

"We don't have to talk about it," she said quietly, laying her cheek against his back for a moment. "I just wanted you to know that I understand."

She did? How could anyone understand?

No, he didn't want to talk about it. Not now. Not if he hoped to keep Eric out of their relationship as much as possible. But he felt the defeat of that moment all over again. Just like his brother, the man had wanted to die. But he'd done something different than Mark. He'd taken a hostage—his own ex-wife.

Maybe J.T. couldn't have talked him down. But he'd been making progress in getting the man to put away his weapon, when the rookie Eric rushed the situation, too much in need of being in charge rather than finding another solution. Startled when Eric moved in on him, the man shoved his ex-wife away, turned his gun on Eric. J.T. had to shoot.

An internal investigation cleared both Eric and J.T., because the man left behind a note announcing his intent to end his miserable life, apologizing to whichever officer pulled the trigger. Still, a senseless death in J.T.'s mind, a desperate solution to an almost hopeless situation. Because of Eric he would never know whether it had been completely hopeless. Would never have a chance to find out.

He couldn't stay on the job after that, especially not with Eric as a partner. And to request a change meant explaining things he didn't want to explain. So he quit. Sold his house. Hit the road. Saw California. Then ended up in Lost and Found because he was drawn to the name, like so many before him.

Fate.

"You're going to wash off three layers of skin," Gina said from behind him, pulling him out of his reminiscences. "I'm sorry I mentioned it. I had promised myself that I wouldn't bring it up. It's a bad memory for you."

Yes. Bad. The worst, because it symbolized failure. "We couldn't avoid it forever." It was a connection, after all, between Eric and him—with her in the middle by default.

"Something else I'd like to bring up, though," she said. "Then the past can die, as far as I'm concerned. Yours *and* mine."

He held himself rigid.

"When you came to me, trying to get me to change my mind about marrying Eric—"

"Not change your mind, but to slow down. There wasn't a reason to rush it."

"Yes. Can you look at me, please?"

He turned around. She laid her hands on his chest.

"When I told you I hated you—" she swallowed "—I didn't. My feelings for you were way too complicated to sum up in any one sentence. I hated myself for how I felt around you. And I hated myself for accepting Eric's proposal when I knew I wasn't ready. I needed a target, and you showed up at the right moment, saying the wrong things."

He cupped her face. "You were so young. And passionate about life."

"Too passionate. Too much in a hurry. I wanted children, my own family. I vowed to love each of them the same, to shower attention on all of them, so they would know how loved they were. So they would never have to wonder. Like I did," she finished in a whisper. "But it was no excuse for how I treated you. I shouldn't have taken out my frustrations on you."

Her gaze turned insistent. "I did love him. It's important that you know that, even if it hurts a little. I wouldn't have been pathetic enough to marry him without loving him. And Joey will know that his father was a good man, that he would've been proud of his son."

J.T. had gotten stuck on the need she'd voiced again to have children, a lot of them. Enough, apparently, to start her own baseball team.

Tell her you can't. Tell her. Stop it now, if it's going to be stopped at all.

"Gina." Her name. Just her name, then no more. The confession wouldn't break out of its prison, even with the key in his hand. He didn't want to crush her dreams, not after all she'd been through.

No choice, though. No damn choice. The whole truth, nothing but the truth. Anything less would be an insult.

He tuned back in to what she was saying.

"It was a love born of rebellion and dreams, which happened to coincide with his," she said, grasping his wrists. "I see that now. And I need to remember the best about him, so that I don't ever think of my marriage to him as a mistake, for my own peace of mind." Her soul opened up in her eyes, then. "But what I feel for you is so much deeper and stronger."

He wrapped her close. *One more night. Just let me have one more night.*

It was cowardly of him and selfish. But he needed her tonight, more than ever. He deserved to celebrate his birthday, for a change.

Tomorrow he would tell her, though, without fail.

As his present to himself, he carried her into the bedroom and unwrapped her like a priceless gift, rediscovering her, layer by layer. By sight and scent and sound. By touch. And a warm honey taste.

The images lingered long after she'd fallen asleep in his arms, naked and entwined, a little sigh escaping her now and then as she slept.

He brooded through the night. Fell asleep finally but dreamed, grotesque visions that made no sense, then he awakened to her soothing him, comforting caresses that turned bold and hot. Daring. Provocative. Tormenting.

Then, satisfaction at last.

Followed by a fear stronger than any he'd known.

The patrons of Belle's Diner buzzed with news that Gina had picked up the gauntlet Belle had thrown down. In this case it was an oven mitt, but the ceremonial effect was the same, Belle assured everyone. The event would be held a week from Wednesday, at the end of the city council meeting, in the empty storefront about to turn library. Three pies each, because the number of council volunteers would undoubtedly increase for one night. Free pie brought out the community spirit, Mayor Taylor said, a twinkle in his eye. He would draw up an official document announcing the Rules of Engagement.

J.T. heard about it everywhere he went, enjoyed the fun everyone was having with the challenge. He was about to lock up for the night when Gina, Winnie, Deputy and the baby came in.

"Joey and I are going to hitch a ride home with you," Gina said, jostling a fussy Joey. "We're pooped, but the library looks great. Twelve people showed up! We got all the bookshelves painted."

He took the baby from her and talked to him. After a few seconds Joey screwed up his face and stared hard at J.T., quieting.

"How does he do that?" Gina said to Winnie in amazement.

"It's a guy thing," J.T. said. Winnie had yet to speak to him, but she and Gina were either ignoring the issue or had gotten past it, because Winnie was flinging daggers in his direction only. He grabbed a spare set of keys from his desk drawer and tossed them to Gina. "Why don't you drive home, and I'll walk with Joey. I don't think he's gonna be happy being buckled in the car seat, even for that distance."

"Can I turn on the siren?" She laughed. "Guess not. But thanks. That'll give me a head start to make dinner."

"I'll fix dinner," he said. "Go relax in a hot bath."

"Well, I can't pass up that offer." She hugged Winnie. "It was fun today."

The phone rang just as Gina left. Winnie stayed, perusing the Wanted posters as he took a report from the sheriff's office, jotting notes while cradling the baby and the telephone. She had something to say, obviously, and wasn't going to leave until she said it.

He hung up the phone, then slid the paper into the top drawer and locked it. And waited.

Winnie stopped wandering. "This was quite a change for you, wasn't it," she said, her eyes as cool as her voice, "coming from L.A. to here."

He reminded himself he should be grateful to her for inadvertently sending Gina his way. And to be honest, he'd come to tolerate the woman well enough. "A good change."

"You don't miss the action?"

"Not for a second."

"You've probably never had to use your gun."

"No." *Come on, Winnie. What do you want?*

"I imagine that's a relief."

"A cop never likes to shoot."

"If it happened, though? Would you run away again?"

His blood turned icy. Okay. He understood now. "Run away?"

"Like before. You quit the force because you shot that man, right?"

"I resigned for several reasons. That was one."

Joey started to fuss, probably feeling the tension. Deputy moved between them and Winnie, his ears back.

"My son told us what happened. So tragic."

"Yes."

"I thought it odd, though, that you were the one with the experience, yet he's the one who didn't panic."

What? *What?*

"Whatever prompted you to force that man's hand? Eric said he'd almost talked him down. He wondered why you hadn't waited for the hostage negotiator."

I had! Eric jumped the gun. Not me!

Wait, he thought. If Winnie thinks this—does Gina?

At his silence, Winnie smiled slightly. "I'm only looking out for my son's wife and child."

Her son's wife and child. As if he needed a reminder.

"Someone has to," she added.

Me. I'm going to look out for them.

"Gina brought it up today. She feels so sorry for you. You know, what a painful memory it must be, and all."

The words hit their target, a straight arrow into the bull's-eye of his pride. No wonder Gina had been sympathetic and so hesitant to discuss the event. She felt sorry for him—and she believed him incompetent.

He couldn't refute Eric's version of the story without looking like a jerk. Blame the dead? Right. The truth had died with Eric.

Joey let out a howl. Deputy growled at Winnie, who stared him down. He backed off, sat tensely.

Comforting the baby, J.T. tried to come up with the right words to clear his name without muddying Eric's. None came. Yet silence would only give credence to Winnie's words.

A string of curses filled his head. Gina *pitied* him? She thought him unfit as a police officer? How could she marry a man like that? *Why* would she?

"You've had your say," he said to Winnie. "And I need to get Joey home."

She stared at him, as if waiting for him to add something. When he didn't, she sighed, said good night and left.

J.T. tucked the baby against his shoulder, his cheek resting on the downy head, and sang to him, a lullaby he'd heard Gina sing every day for a month now. The words came, awkward and hesitant, without thought, without emotion, comforting himself more than the baby.

Joey calmed.

J.T. imploded, his hopes and dreams reduced to rubble. He had no future with Gina and the baby, yet he couldn't ask her to leave. He needed her to know the truth, yet he couldn't tell her without tarnishing the memory of a man she loved. Nor would Winnie ever accept J.T. being responsible for her only grandchild. That was clear.

Everyone loses, yet no one wins.

Thirteen

Gina heard the back door open, then Joey crying so hard his voice quavered. He'd worked himself into a frenzy that even J.T. couldn't soothe. She sat up in the bathtub as they approached. Her milk let down. She smiled at J.T., who didn't smile back.

"Is the bathwater too warm for him to join you?" he asked.

"You'll have to test it. I'm used to it."

He managed to push up his sleeve, then dipped a wrist in. "Seems okay. I'll strip him down."

He was gone before she could say thanks. Ignoring the little warning bell that rang in her head, she sank to chin level again, warming her chest.

J.T. swooped in, handed over the wriggling, naked baby, then left, muttering something about dinner.

Bells pealed a little louder. It wasn't like him not to sit with her while she nursed. Last night all three of them had squeezed into the tub together. She'd kind of expected him to join them now.

Joey nursed frantically for a few minutes before he relaxed. She kissed his head, toyed with his hair. "You had a big day, didn't you? It's tough having everyone dote on you."

He smiled at her.

"Charmer. You know exactly how to get what you want, don't you?" She couldn't hear kitchen noises, but she assumed J.T. was there, fixing dinner. She dragged a finger along Joey's arm. "So, what do you think, Mr. Smarty Pants. Is J.T. going to propose to us?"

"Spaghetti okay?" J.T. stepped into the room.

She heated up from more than the bathwater. "Um, that's fine. But there's no hurry, is there? Come sit with us for a while."

"No time. I've got to go back to the office after dinner."

Off he went, without once looking below her chin.

Notre Dame's bells had never clanged so loud as the ones going off in her head. He'd heard her talking to Joey. She was sure of it. Plus, he'd already been acting strangely. Dread tiptoed in.

She had a reprieve, though, until Joey was bathed and dressed. She didn't hurry the task as the scent of basil and oregano drifted from the kitchen, but she wondered how she was supposed to have an appetite.

Her hands shook; her heart thudded. All day she'd been ignoring how cool he'd been at breakfast. Not cold, but distant. She couldn't imagine why, not after the night they'd shared. He'd recemented some walls between them, though. At first she'd chalked it up to the aftermath of his reliving his memories, then she'd thought maybe things were moving a little too fast for comfort for him.

"He's just adjusting," she whispered to Joey, who'd dropped to sleep as soon as he was bundled up. "And he's not a man of many words. He'll come around."

Still, she stalled leaving the bedroom until he called out that dinner was ready.

They pushed food around their plates. She saw him glance at her still-full dinner plate as often as she looked at his.

"Why do you have to go back to the office?" she asked at last.

"A conference call."

"How long will you be gone?"

"Am I punching a time clock at home now?"

Startled, she locked her hands in her lap, felt her napkin slip to the floor, a lead blanket on her feet. "Of course not. I just wondered."

He rubbed a hand down his face. "I'm sorry."

"It's okay—"

"No." He shoved his plate aside. "No, Gina, it's not okay. Nothing's okay."

Fear smacked an open hand against her chest.

"You're sitting there wondering if I overheard what you said to the baby. About me proposing."

Her throat closed, intensifying the pain streaking from her heart.

"I don't want you to have any illusions," he said flatly. "I thought you understood that I have no plans to be married."

He wouldn't look her in the eye, which gave her a measured dose of courage, counteracting the crushing pain. She dug into her memory. "You said it wouldn't be easy being married to you. That's different. And entirely true," she added, anger coming to her rescue, bringing her voice back. "And having children has never been high on your list. Did I get that quote right?" She didn't wait for an answer. "I already come with a child. Double jeopardy."

She'd been hoping against hope that her fears were all in her head, that she couldn't read him as well as she thought. Fool.

Her love for him was in the tendermost stage of all, easy to blossom and easy to crush, but she was a mature woman now, with a child to think of, not dependent on anyone but themselves. Better now than later.

She pushed herself up, grateful her legs locked. "We'll get out of your hair."

"You don't have to go." He swore. "I'm not kicking you out."

"Why would I stay? You still want me to warm your bed or something?" How could she have made the same mistake? First Eric, now J.T. To be that wrong twice—

No. She'd watched him with Joey. Been the beneficiary of his tenderness—and his passion. He couldn't fake that. He just couldn't. She pressed her palms to her eyes. A jumble of emotions zoomed in and around her, creating chaos in her head. She plucked one question out of the pandemonium.

"What's really going on here?" she asked, then was struck by a new thought. "What are you afraid of?"

"You've been hurt enough—"

"Oh, you got that right, pal. And if you hadn't overheard my...my—" *fondest wish* "—speculation with Joey, how long would you have continued to use me?"

He shoved himself up, towered over her. "Look. You knew from the start that I wasn't the man for you.

Too many years separate us. We want different things. I can't have children.''

''Can't?'' Something flickered in his eyes, then died out. *Can't?* The word dangled in the air between them.

''Don't want them,'' he amended, too fast.

He said can't. ''You took such good care of my son.''

''He's a baby! What was I supposed to do, ignore him?''

I can not be that wrong. What am I missing? What clue are you keeping from me? She needed her mind to clear so she could sort the facts.

He looked at his watch. ''I have to go.''

''Fine. Run away.'' She saw him flinch. What chord had she struck there? Too many clues and not enough time to analyze them.

''You don't have to leave yet, Gina.''

''Why not? You found your grail, after all. Your quest to toss me on the pool table and take me has been fulfilled. I'm terribly sorry you had to use a bed, but at least your curiosity has been satisfied.''

''Not satisfied,'' he said, then clamped his mouth shut.

She fell back a step. ''I didn't satisfy you?''

''That's not what I mean. Hell. I meant that two nights weren't enough to satisfy. God. I'm making a mess of this.''

''Am I supposed to feel better knowing you still want me? That it's always only been physical?''

He wrapped his hands around her arms, holding her without hurting, but forcing her to look at him and listen.

''Here are some facts,'' he said, his mouth hard, his eyes no longer golden. ''One, yes, I've wanted you since the moment I saw you. Two, making love with you was better than my fantasies. Three, I liked having you and the baby here. But, four, I am not husband material.'' He said each word distinctly, as if she were slow-witted. "And you want a family, desperately.''

"Five,'' she said quietly. "Eric will always be between us.''

His mouth tightened impossibly. "That, too.''

"Why? Aside from going after me when you wouldn't—'' she took a chance she was right on that "—what did he do to you?''

His eyes went blank, his body rigid, but he said nothing. She'd gone beyond some unspoken boundary, something to do with Eric.

"I wish you'd been honest with me before I bared my soul,'' she said, the words painful. *Before I pried open my chest and handed you my heart to keep with you forever.* She lifted her chin a little higher. "I'll sleep in the guest room. And tomorrow we'll go.''

"You don't—''

She interrupted him with a gesture. "You know, it's going to be very hard to trust a man again, because I trusted you not only with my life, but with my child's life. There's no higher compliment I could pay you. To be that wrong...''

Tears, which had been welling up slowly as her heart wept, pressed at her eyes. She debated whether to let him see, this man who said he would protect her with his life. He'd held her son even before she had. He'd changed diapers and walked the floor with him. Kissed his little foot. Soothed him when no one else could. Made him laugh. Made her happy. Been her partner.

Lies.

"I took off my ring for you,'' she whispered. Then

she pulled away and left him, hoping he hurt half as much as she did, knowing it wasn't humanly possible.

He didn't go home, but sat in his car where he could see the house, in case she left in the middle of the night. She didn't. But lights were on until well past two o'clock, then at six-thirty she came out the back door, a grocery sack in each hand, which she loaded into her car, then returned for more. Deputy followed her, danced around her, barking occasionally. She ignored him. J.T. figured she saw *him,* though. He wasn't attempting to hide.

Winnie drove up, pulled in behind her. They hugged and went into the house together, arm in arm.

After a while they came out, this time with the baby. When Gina climbed into the back seat to buckle him in, J.T. left his car and walked the hundred yards between them, his gaze fixed on her.

She shooed the dog away, then shut the car door and waited, stiff-backed and silent. Winnie headed for her car, passing by him. At least she didn't attempt to rub his nose in her triumph. "Thanks for taking good care of my family," she said, surprising him.

He supposed that being the winner meant she could be generous. She started her car and backed down the driveway, then waited at the bottom.

"So, this is it," he said to Gina. Her eyes weren't puffy from crying, but the sparkle was gone.

"Guess so."

Her blasé response irked him. *Damn it, Gina. You pity me. You think I'm a lousy cop who's hiding out here because I couldn't cut it in the big city. You believed that lying bastard you married. Why didn't you know him better than that?*

Why don't you know *me* better than that?

He shoved a hand through his hair. He'd been over and over it in his mind during the long, cold hours. Nothing had changed. Nothing would.

"Will you let me know that you got home safely?"

"Your job is done, Chief."

Her chin quivered. His heart hurt.

He opened the back door of the car and knelt on the seat. The baby was awake, his eyes focused on the swaying trees outside the back window. J.T. waited for him to see him. He did. And he smiled, big and bright.

J.T.'s chest swelled, his eyes burned. "Hey, JoJo."

The smile faded into that serious frown he got sometimes.

"You're one lucky boy, you know that?"

The smile again.

"Take good care of her, okay?"

Bouncing one leg, he smiled a little broader.

J.T. backed out of the car and shut the door, then faced her, his soul on fire, a prelude to the hell he was about to live in. Her arms were folded across her stomach, as effective as an iron shield.

"Be happy," he said, then scooped up the dog and headed to the house, not looking back when the engine started. Or when the tires crushed bits of gravel down the driveway. Or when the engine shifted from reverse to forward. Accelerated. Then faded.

Well, Mark, what do you say now? I put her needs above mine, even though it's killing me. Someone else can give her children, someone who won't be the subject of her pity. Chivalry is not dead. There's your proof.

You put her needs first? came the sarcastic response. *Your armor's rusted shut, brother.*

Fourteen

After wandering around the house for an hour, J.T. figured he'd be better off at work. He needed to deal with all the baby gear he'd borrowed for her, but not today, not after his chest constricted when he set the rocking chair in motion. And he couldn't climb into a bed that smelled like her, so he stripped the sheets and dumped them in the washing machine.

His hand hesitated over the dial. He lifted the lid and snatched a pillowcase from on top, the flowery-scented one. Folding it neatly, he drew it to his nose, then set it carefully on the dryer. He punched the start button with unnecessary force, grabbed his jacket and hurried out of the house.

Jamming his hands in his pockets, he made the long walk back to his car, Deputy trailing instead of leading, and scanning the countryside as he went, looking confused every time J.T. turned around to look at him.

Great. Guilt on top of misery. He wondered how long it would take for the dog to forgive him.

He wondered how long it would take to forget her.

Cars were parked in front of Belle's, otherwise the town was still quiet. He needed coffee, but not company. He could make his rounds, end up at Max's for breakfast, or Brynne's, but dismissed the thought.

"This isn't like you," she'd said to him the last time, probably the most personal remark she'd made to him. "Or maybe it is, J.T. Did you think of that?"

Yeah, he'd thought about it plenty, for all the good it did him. He couldn't deny Gina had changed him.

He settled on making a pot of coffee in his office. Deputy refused to come in with him, but took off up the street. J.T. hoped it wasn't to chase Mrs. Foley's cat. He was in no mood to rescue it.

Waiting for the coffee to brew, he sat at his desk, pillowed his head on his arms and closed his eyes…

The dog scratched at the door, whining.

Groggy, J.T. sat up. "Keep your fur on, mutt." Every muscle aching, he stood, stretched, glanced at his watch. Stared. He'd slept three hours?

Deputy whined again—

No. That wasn't a dog whining. It was a baby crying. And not just any baby.

JoJo.

Gina fluttered a hand at Deputy. "Keep scratching," she whispered, as if he knew what she was saying. Joey built up a little more steam. She was going to have to give up soon and feed him. *Come on, J.T. Open up.*

Bam. The door flew open and he looked out as Deputy ran back to sit at her feet. She leaned against the railing outside Mrs. Foley's shop, trying to look unaffected, knowing her future depended on how she handled this opportunity.

He moved like a sheriff in the Old West, a slow mosey to his walk, but not fooling her. He was gathering his defenses.

He stopped a couple of feet from her. She hoped she wasn't making a mistake. She hoped she had him all figured out. If not, she had only dragged out the inevitable—for both of them.

But she'd heard him call her son JoJo. It gave her more hope than anything he'd said. It was personal and sweet. Loving.

"Did you have car trouble?" he asked above the baby noise.

"Nope."

Joey hushed, turned his head. Hunted. J.T. moved to where the baby could see him, although he didn't attempt to hold him, as he always had.

"Why are you here?" he asked, his expression bland.

"I live here."

His jaw turned to granite; he narrowed his eyes. "What?" Low. Dangerous.

She shivered, liking the sensation.

A pickup truck rumbled past, the driver beeping and waving. She waved back.

He eyed the truck suspiciously. "What are Barney's boys doing with the rocking chair and bassinet?"

"Taking them to Mrs. Foley's house. We moved in."

"You can't do that."

"Show me the law that says I can't."

"Gina." His voice held that all-too-patient, all-too-condescending tone she'd heard from men forever.

"Are you telling me to get outa Dodge, Chief?"

He ignored her attempt at humor. "It would be too painful, and you know it."

"For me or for you?"

His mouth drew into a tight line.

"In case you forgot, I've been challenged to a bake-off. I don't duck my commitments."

"Unlike me? Is that what you're saying?"

"If the guilt fits…"

"Guilt?"

A few people gathered, the distance respectful but probably within hearing range. J.T. issued a "back off" order with his eyes. Nobody budged. Gina looked at the ground until the need to laugh faded.

"Come to my office, Gina."

"Joey's hungry."

"So? Feed him inside."

"I can't," she said quietly. "Not anymore."

Hurt darkened his expression, but she wouldn't back down. She knew what he was afraid of. "If you want to talk, Chief, give me a call to schedule some time."

"Schedule some—"

"I'll see if I can fit you in."

"You'll see if—"

"I've got library work to do, after all. And Winnie wants to start coordinating the Meals on Wheels."

He looked increasingly dazed—until that moment. "Winnie's still here?"

"She has commitments, too, you know." She soothed Joey, who'd waited long enough. "One of the Cochran boys will return your house key when they're done. I forgot to give it back to you."

"Forgot? Don't insult me." He turned on his heel, then stopped.

A small mob had congregated now and was listening, fascinated. Even Max.

J.T. turned back to Gina, came almost nose to nose with her. "I never figured you for a vengeful person."

"I'm not," she whispered, standing on tiptoe, bringing her mouth close to his ear. She hoped she was right, that he was ready to hear the words. "I'm in love. And I figured out why you won't marry me."

With that she stepped around him and into Mrs. Foley's shop, closing the door with a precisely controlled click.

His bed felt about the size of a football field without her. Even Deputy had packed his bags and left home. Well, maybe that was an exaggeration, J.T. thought, trying to be fair. He didn't have bags, after all. But three days ago he'd carried his food dish all the way to Mrs. Foley's, who'd welcomed him with a "Scram!" only to give in when he looked so completely pathetic.

Or so J.T. had heard from Max. He wouldn't know, personally. Gina hadn't returned any of his six calls as yet.

I'm in love.

Her words danced around him, sometimes with the slow beauty of a waltz, sometimes with the heat of a tango. If only love was enough.

And JoJo had taken on a mythic role, being the first baby born in Lost and Found in thirty-eight years. Everyone decided he was a symbol of renewal for the town, which, admittedly, had stagnated. The population was aging. If anyone with children did move in, those children eventually grew up and moved on.

But a child born in Lost and Found would feel a

stronger commitment to staying, wouldn't he? Or so the speculation went.

It was an awesome responsibility to place on a baby. Someone needed to make sure the expectations didn't become overwhelming. If he—they—stayed on.

J.T. punched his pillow. No one talked to him directly about what happened, but he heard bits of gossip. The only person he wanted to talk to was avoiding him.

Well, there was one other—Mark—but even he had stopped talking. J.T. had taken his brother's photograph out of the drawer and set it on the mantel in the living room, knowing he wouldn't hear Mark again. The voice in his head hadn't been his brother but himself, trying to keep him alive. The revelation hurt as much as it helped. He hadn't known he was capable of that kind of bitterness.

Loneliness swamped him. A couple of months ago he'd been perfectly happy. Content…

And I figured out why you won't marry me.

Hell. She sure knew how to get to him.

He threw back the blankets, pulled on some clothes and headed out on foot. If he couldn't sleep, he might as well check that everyone had locked up for the night. But his legs took him without a pause to Mrs. Foley's house on the other side of downtown. The lights were out. He looked at his watch. A little past midnight.

He knew which room Gina slept in. Had made it his business to find out.

A pebble crunched underfoot. He stooped, picked it up, crept closer to the house. He took aim, tossed it at her window. *Plick.*

He waited. No response.

Hell. What was it about her that reduced him to adolescence? His jealousy had gotten way out of hand.

He blew out a breath, the cold air fogging in front of his face. As long as J.T. was being honest with himself, he had to admit the mistakes he made with Eric.

Scrounging, he found two more stones and hefted them. Too heavy? Maybe. But he wanted her to wake up. He tossed them, one after another. The window opened and she stuck her head out.

"Are you drunk?"

He laughed. He didn't know why, but it wasn't what he'd expected to hear, and it made him happy.

"I'm coming up," he said, not waiting for an answer. He jumped to grab a low, thick limb of a tree, dangled for a second, then hefted himself up onto it. Standing, he moved to a higher and longer limb leading to her room. Her hands were smashed against her mouth, like she might scream otherwise.

She wore his shirt.

He stopped for a second, appreciating the sight, then he inched along the sturdy branch, threw one leg over the sill and slid into the room, landing with a soft thud.

"Guess all that experience getting the damn cat down came in handy, after all," he said with a grin.

"What are you doing here?" she whispered, sending cautious looks toward her door.

"Your—"

"Shh."

"—social secretary couldn't seem to find an opening for me. I figured maybe your calendar would be free about this time of night. Can I stay?"

"If you're quiet." She frowned. "My social secretary?"

"Winnie. Do you ever answer the phone yourself?"

"Well…"

"I thought not. Where's JoJo?"

"I was informed that it was time for him to sleep in his own room."

"And you obeyed?"

She rubbed her arms. "It was hard at first. I woke up a lot, listening for his breathing, until I realized he wasn't here. I'm adjusting."

He shrugged out of his jacket and draped it around her, not letting his hands linger. "Get back under the covers. You're freezing."

She scurried to the bed and climbed in. "No fireplace in here. And Mrs. Foley doesn't believe in heating above fifty degrees at night."

"Come home with me." The words slipped out, startling him as much as her. He tucked his hands in his back pockets.

"Not without marriage," she said after a minute. "And you won't marry me because of your brother. Because of his illness. Because it's believed to have a certain genetic connection."

"How do you know that?"

"I researched it."

"Then you know that the likelihood is strong that I would pass that gene along."

"Stronger that you won't."

He stepped closer. "I can't take that chance. I lived it, Gina. I lived it. To put another human being through that? My own child?" He sat on the bed finally, facing her, the old mattress dipping low.

"But they're coming up with better ways of helping manic-depressives all the time. And we'd be more alert to the signals than most and get help sooner and make sure they followed the doctor's orders. Your brother had an extreme case. It's worth the risk, J.T. It is."

"Not to me. If you'd been there, you'd agree. And

the chances are greater of me carrying a gene, because we were twins. I was just lucky enough not to develop it yet.''

"Yet?"

"There's still a chance."

"Every couple takes a chance when they have a baby. It's called faith, J.T. Sometimes babies are born with problems. If that happened, we would deal with it, right?" She got to her knees, reached for him. "I love you."

He almost said he loved her, too. He almost asked if she'd be willing to adopt. Then he remembered the lie that Eric had told. The big lie. She would never have complete faith in him to protect them. Like Winnie, she would always be afraid he would run when things got tough.

Too many strikes against them.

Why had he thought otherwise, even for a second? Why had he let himself hope? He was hurting both of them. Again.

Damn it. Why hadn't she just left town like she was supposed to?

The bedroom door creaked open, silhouetting a woman in the hall. Winnie.

"Gina? Are you okay?" Her hand moved along the wall.

"Don't turn on the—"

A bright overhead light came on.

"Lights," Gina finished lamely.

"We're having a private conversation," J.T. said over his shoulder to Winnie, not in the mood to play games with her.

"Tough."

He turned around. She shut the door and walked up to the bed.

"I have something to say."

"Winnie," Gina said, ducking back under the covers and looking back and forth between J.T. and her mother-in-law. "This isn't a good time."

"This is the only time." She clasped her hands at her waist. "I was wrong about you, J.T."

"About which thing?"

"You get smart-mouthed with me and I won't say this. Believe me, you want to hear it."

J.T. sent a glance Gina's way, but said nothing.

"The other day in your office I repeated something Eric had told me, which I've since discovered I was wrong about. I saw something in your eyes..." She stopped, took a breath. "This is hard for me to say. I knew my son well enough to know he exaggerated, sometimes even lied, because he always needed to be right. And I'm afraid his father and I indulged him too much in his life."

Her gaze flickered to Gina. "I called his former captain and asked for the straight story. He pussyfooted around the answer, so I knew something was up. When I explained my suspicions, he finally told me everything. Gina, Eric lied to us. He said it was J.T.'s fault that man got shot. But it was Eric's."

Gina stared at J.T. This is what had been bothering him? This was what had made him push her away? She'd been so sure it was about having babies. *Not* having babies.

"Is that true?" she asked him.

He looked into the distance, his eyes unfocused, his expression painful to watch.

Finally he ran a hand down his face. "It's more complicated than that. It's true that Eric rushed the situation. Rookies sometimes do, because they haven't learned how to control the adrenaline. In all fairness, though, the shooting may have been inevitable. An internal investigation cleared him. Both of us."

"You didn't correct me, even when I basically called you a coward," Winnie said, her voice quavering. "I accused you of running away. Hiding out here."

Oh, no. Gina wrapped a hand around J.T.'s fist. Winnie couldn't have accused him of anything worse. A coward? He would lay down his life to protect.

Her mother-in-law stood a little taller. "You let me have my illusions about my son. You are an honorable man, J.T. Ryker. And I'm proud to know you." She put a hand on his shoulder. "I can't imagine a better father for my grandson than you. If you can't work things out with Gina, so be it. But don't let it be because of me. Or Eric. Joey's who matters. He deserves a family. Now, I'll leave you alone to continue your conversation."

J.T. stopped her. "Thank you."

"Shielding people from the truth isn't always the best way to go, J.T. We women—" she tossed a glance Gina's way "—we're tougher than we look."

"I won't make the same mistake."

"Good."

They were left with a quiet room and a lot to think about.

"That's why you hated Eric," Gina said, breaking the silence. "He went against everything you believed in, every reason you became a cop."

"We really did have different philosophies about the job. But to be honest, I was harder on him because I was jealous that he could have you and I couldn't."

Since the incident, I've had nightmares about shooting the man, except that just as the bullet strikes, he turns into Mark.''

She pressed her hands to his face, forcing him to look at her. ''All this time?''

He nodded. ''I'd finally stopped dreaming about it when you showed up. Then everything came back.''

''You blamed me?''

''I blamed Eric. Always. It was easier to blame him than to deal with my own failure. I failed Mark. I failed in my goal to prevent the same thing from happening to someone else.''

''Do you really believe you could have done anything differently?''

''No.'' His gaze pierced hers. ''That's what I'm telling you. I finally know I couldn't.''

''Eric was a good man, deep down,'' she whispered, her throat hurting. ''I have to believe that.''

''He had to be a good man. You loved him.''

Hold me. Please hold me. ''I love you more. Much, much more.''

''He gave you a son.'' He finally touched her, his hands cupping her face, then her shoulders, her face again. ''But I'd be honored to raise him.''

She threw herself into his arms.

''I love you, Gina. Please will you marry me?''

''Oh, yes. Yes!'' She drew back. ''No.''

''No?''

''Not without knowing your name.''

One side of his mouth tipped up. ''It's Jasper Thelonius.''

''Oh.'' She toyed with his shirt buttons. ''Um, you're not set on having a junior named after you, are you?''

"Gina." He laughed. "Just Teasing."

"Can I say *good?*" She poked a finger at his chest. "Well, what is it?"

"Jeffrey Tyler."

"Jeff. I can see you as a Jeff."

"Could even manage a junior with that one, I suppose," he said, all of a sudden interested in the buttons on *her* shirt. He slipped one out. Another.

She grabbed his hand, stopping him. *The million-dollar question, J.T.* "Does that mean we're going to have children?"

His gaze fell tenderly on her. "I guess I'll have to learn to have faith."

Joy burst inside her. She would've found other ways—adoption or technology, but this felt right. Life didn't come with guarantees. "I'll help you. I love you so much."

"I love you more."

She lost herself in his long, luxurious kiss. Found herself in his powerful embrace. Lost and found—for the rest of her life.

She could live with that.

*   *   *   *   *

COMING NEXT MONTH

#1303 BACHELOR DOCTOR—Barbara Boswell
Man of the Month

He was brilliant, handsome—and couldn't keep his mind off nurse
Callie Sheely! No one had ever captured Dr. Trey Weldon's attention
like Callie, but she insisted their relationship would never work. Could
Trey convince Callie otherwise with a soul-stirring seduction…?

#1304 MIDNIGHT FANTASY—Ann Major
Body & Soul

Tag rescued Claire when she was in dire peril—and then showed her
the delights of true fantasy. Could this very real man of her dreams
save Claire from even greater danger—marriage to the wrong man?

#1305 WIFE FOR HIRE—Amy J. Fetzer
Wife, Inc.

What horse breeder Nash Rayburn needed was a temporary wife. What
he got was Hayley Albright, his former lover and soon-to-be doctor.
But Hayley still carried a torch for Nash. Could she rekindle *his* love—
this time permanently?

#1306 RIDE A WILD HEART—Peggy Moreland
Texas Grooms

Bronc rider Pete Dugan always knew that he was not cut out to be a
family man—then Carol Benson walked back into his life. Carol had
commitment written all over her, but when she revealed her long-held
secret, would Pete be ready to say "I do"?

#1307 BLOOD BROTHERS—Anne McAllister and Lucy Gordon
2-in-1 Original Stories

Double trouble! That's what you got when cousins Montana cowboy
Gabe McBride and British lord Randall Stanton traded places. What
Gabe and Randall got was the challenge of their lives—wooing the
women of their hearts. Because to win Claire McBride and Frederika
Crossman, these two blood brothers would need to exert all their
British pluck and cowboy try!

#1308 COWBOY FOR KEEPS—Kristi Gold

Single mom Dana Landry cared only about catering to the special
needs of her daughter. Then cowboy Will Baker taught Dana she had
to take care of *her* needs, as well—and he was just the man to help.
But when the night was over, would Will still want to be Dana's
cowboy for keeps?

CMN0600

Multi-*New York Times* bestselling author

NORA ROBERTS

knew from the first how to capture readers' hearts.
Celebrate the 20th Anniversary of Silhouette Books
with this special 2-in-1 edition containing her fabulous
first book and the sensational sequel.

Coming in June

IRISH HEARTS

Adelia Cunnane's fiery temper sets proud, powerful horse
breeder Travis Grant's heart aflame and he resolves to
make this wild *Irish Thoroughbred* his own.

Erin McKinnon accepts wealthy Burke Logan's loveless
proposal, but can this ravishing *Irish Rose* win her
hard-hearted husband's love?

Also available in June from
Silhouette Special Edition (SSE #1328)

IRISH REBEL

In this brand-new sequel to *Irish Thoroughbred*, Travis and
Adelia's innocent but strong-willed daughter Keeley discovers
love in the arms of a charming Irish rogue with a talent for
horses...and romance.

Where love comes alive™

Silhouette® Desire®

Proudly presents

Blood Brothers
(SD #1307)

Two great love stories… One super read…
by top authors

Anne McAllister
and Lucy Gordon

Double trouble! That's what you get when
Montana cowboy Gabe McBride and his cousin
British lord Randall Stanton trade places. What
Gabe and Randall got was the challenge of their
lives as they attempted to woo two
unforgettable women—with their British pluck
and cowboy try!

*Don't miss this irresistible romance…
available July 2000 at your favorite retail outlet.*

Silhouette®
Where love comes alive™

SILHOUETTE'S 20TH ANNIVERSARY CONTEST
OFFICIAL RULES
NO PURCHASE NECESSARY TO ENTER

1. To enter, follow directions published in the offer to which you are responding. Contest begins 1/1/00 and ends on 8/24/00 (the "Promotion Period"). Method of entry may vary. Mailed entries must be postmarked by 8/24/00, and received by 8/31/00.

2. During the Promotion Period, the Contest may be presented via the Internet. Entry via the Internet may be restricted to residents of certain geographic areas that are disclosed on the Web site. To enter via the Internet, if you are a resident of a geographic area in which Internet entry is permissible, follow the directions displayed on-line, including typing your essay of 100 words or fewer telling us "Where In The World Your Love Will Come Alive." On-line entries must be received by 11:59 p.m. Eastern Standard time on 8/24/00. Limit one e-mail entry per person, household and e-mail address per day, per presentation. If you are a resident of a geographic area in which entry via the Internet is permissible, you may, in lieu of submitting an entry on-line, enter by mail, by hand-printing your name, address, telephone number and contest number/name on an 8"x 11" plain piece of paper and telling us in 100 words or fewer "Where In The World Your Love Will Come Alive," and mailing via first-class mail to: Silhouette 20th Anniversary Contest, (in the U.S.) P.O. Box 9069, Buffalo, NY 14269-9069; (In Canada) P.O. Box 637, Fort Erie, Ontario, Canada L2A 5X3. Limit one 8"x 11" mailed entry per person, household and e-mail address per day. On-line and/or 8"x 11" mailed entries received from persons residing in geographic areas in which Internet entry is not permissible will be disqualified. No liability is assumed for lost, late, incomplete, inaccurate, nondelivered or misdirected mail, or misdirected e-mail, for technical, hardware or software failures of any kind, lost or unavailable network connection, or failed, incomplete, garbled or delayed computer transmission or any human error which may occur in the receipt or processing of the entries in the contest.

3. Essays will be judged by a panel of members of the Silhouette editorial and marketing staff based on the following criteria:

   Sincerity (believability, credibility)—50%

   Originality (freshness, creativity)—30%

   Aptness (appropriateness to contest ideas)—20%

   Purchase or acceptance of a product offer does not improve your chances of winning. In the event of a tie, duplicate prizes will be awarded.

4. All entries become the property of Harlequin Enterprises Ltd., and will not be returned. Winner will be determined no later than 10/31/00 and will be notified by mail. Grand Prize winner will be required to sign and return Affidavit of Eligibility within 15 days of receipt of notification. Noncompliance within the time period may result in disqualification and an alternative winner may be selected. All municipal, provincial, federal, state and local laws and regulations apply. Contest open only to residents of the U.S. and Canada who are 18 years of age or older, and is void wherever prohibited by law. Internet entry is restricted solely to residents of those geographical areas in which Internet entry is permissible. Employees of Torstar Corp., their affiliates, agents and members of their immediate families are not eligible. Taxes on the prizes are the sole responsibility of winners. Entry and acceptance of any prize offered constitutes permission to use winner's name, photograph or other likeness for the purposes of advertising, trade and promotion on behalf of Torstar Corp. without further compensation to the winner, unless prohibited by law. Torstar Corp and D.L. Blair, Inc., their parents, affiliates and subsidiaries, are not responsible for errors in printing or electronic presentation of contest or entries. In the event of printing or other errors which may result in unintended prize values or duplication of prizes, all affected contest materials or entries shall be null and void. If for any reason the Internet portion of the contest is not capable of running as planned, including infection by computer virus, bugs, tampering, unauthorized intervention, fraud, technical failures, or any other causes beyond the control of Torstar Corp. which corrupt or affect the administration, secrecy, fairness, integrity or proper conduct of the contest, Torstar Corp. reserves the right, at its sole discretion, to disqualify any individual who tampers with the entry process and to cancel, terminate, modify or suspend the contest or the Internet portion thereof. In the event of a dispute regarding an on-line entry, the entry will be deemed submitted by the authorized holder of the e-mail account submitted at the time of entry. Authorized account holder is defined as the natural person who is assigned to an e-mail address by an Internet access provider, on-line service provider or other organization that is responsible for arranging e-mail address for the domain associated with the submitted e-mail address.

5. Prizes: Grand Prize—a $10,000 vacation to anywhere in the world. Travelers (at least one must be 18 years of age or older) or parent or guardian (if one traveler is a minor, must sign and return a Release of Liability prior to departure. Travel must be completed by December 31, 2001, and is subject to space and accommodations availability. Two hundred (200) Second Prizes—a two-book limited edition autographed collector set from one of the Silhouette Anniversary authors: Nora Roberts, Diana Palmer, Linda Howard or Annette Broadrick (value $10.00 each set). All prizes are valued in U.S. dollars.

6. For a list of winners (available after 10/31/00, send a self-addressed, stamped envelope to: Harlequin Silhouette 20th Anniversary Winners, P.O. Box 4200, Blair, NE 68009-4200.

Contest sponsored by Torstar Corp., P.O. Box 9042, Buffalo, NY 14269-9042.